# THE CREEPING HOURS

# THE
# CREEPING HOURS

A JOHN JERICHO MYSTERY NOVEL

By HUGH PENTECOST

DODD, MEAD & COMPANY
*NEW YORK*

RED BADGE
MYSTERY

Library of Congress Catalog Card Number: 66-27939

Printed in the United States of America
by Vail-Ballou Press, Inc., Binghamton, N. Y.

# Part I

# One

If Jericho had been working that Friday night and hot, or if there'd been a girl around who was gay and who liked to make love without demanding promises for her future, or if some poor underdog had gotten himself kicked in the stomach, I'd never have gotten him to Tommy Nolan's place. As it was, I found him at his studio in Jefferson Mews in a black, angry mood. It was what I call his "I'll-never-paint-again" mood.

You have to know John Jericho pretty well to understand his volcanic moods. It takes awhile. It takes awhile to get over the impact his personal appearance has on you. He stands six feet six inches tall and weighs a good two hundred and forty pounds without an ounce of extra fat. His thick red hair and his belligerent red beard make him a man you don't pass by without a second look. He's like a Viking warrior out of another age and time.

Jericho is a painter by profession, and his work hangs in many museums and private collections. He's controversial. He paints what he sees and feels like a man on fire. You are swept away by his work or you hate it passionately. There is no such thing as indifference to Jericho. As a human being he is a sucker for the helpless, for the lost causes of individuals and groups. His enthusiasms are enormous; his vitality threatens to sweep you out of the way.

The first time I ever saw Jericho was toward the end of the Korean war. I was in Army Intelligence and he was brought to me to report on a commando raid he'd led behind the enemy lines. He didn't have the beard in those days, and my first impression was of a physical giant with the grace and agility of a ballet dancer. The word on him was that he was a man without fear, which isn't always impressive. It suggests a man without imagination. If you can't imagine danger, it doesn't take courage to face it. I came to know Jericho as the most imaginative man I'd ever encountered. His bright blue eyes could pick up, and retain, more detail in five minutes than the average man can see after hours of careful survey. This ability is what makes him a very great painter.

We are strange opposites, Jericho and I. Perhaps that's what has cemented our friendship for all the years after Korea. I am short and plump and like to sit still and listen. I am a connoisseur of good foods and wines, something of a gourmet. Jericho eats, enormously, to stoke an engine. Meat in quantity, a green vegetable, a slab of bread and

cheese, all washed down by a cheap chianti—that's
cho's choice menu. When it comes to hard liquor, he
drink any man I ever met under the table and show no ap
parent signs of it. My mind is a kind of computer, digest-
ing facts and retaining them for my use as a writer. I am
an objective observer, using what I see and hear to make
my work factually sound. Jericho sees nothing without re-
acting intensely.

It was to Jericho I went the night after Tommy Nolan
died. I went to him ostensibly because he was an artist
with taste and judgment about things artistic. I didn't tell
him that my real reason was I wanted confirmation about
a hunch. My hunch was that Tommy Nolan's much regretted suicide was, in fact, a perfectly executed murder. . . .

Jefferson Mews, in the heart of Greenwich Village in
New York, had once been a group of stables built around
an open court where the rich kept their horses and their
elegant rigs. Eventually, with the arrival of the automo-
bile and the passing of the horse car, the stables had been
converted into apartments and studios, occupied by writ-
ers and artists and a collection of white-collar workers
who found the surroundings "quaint." Greenwich Village
is no longer the home of great revolutionary talents in the
arts. Beatniks and offbeat musicians hover there now, but
the real-estate tycoons are gradually closing in. Modern
apartment houses rise month by month, smothering the
remainder of old private homes and historical landmarks.

5

richo's studio, a two-story room with a north skylight
d a bedroom and kitchenette appended, is primarily a
storage place for his canvases and the hundreds of
sketches he makes on his travels around the world. It is
thoroughly equipped with fluorescent lighting in case he
chooses to work at night. Knowing him as I do, I'm fully
aware that he seldom does anything new in the studio.
When he stays any length of time in New York, it is usually a refresher time between projects. Toward the end of
each of these stays he falls into the Black World. He mut-
ters that he's lost the spark, that he'll never paint again.
He refuses to answer his phone. He insults most of his
friends into leaving him alone.

I know the signs. In a day or two he'll be gone, and the
next news of him will be a card from some faraway place,
scrawled on with a black marking pencil—a message or a
cartoon.

It was a night of hunches for me. I had a hunch about
Tommy Nolan, lying in an undertaking parlor on Lexington Avenue. I had a hunch that Jericho was at the Mews,
in spite of the fact that he hadn't answered his phone for
two hours. I'd called him every fifteen minutes during
that stretch. I took a cab from The Players and walked up
the one flight of stairs to the studio. A strip of bright light
showed under the door. I knocked.

Nothing happened.

I pounded on the door. "Open up," I shouted.

The door was jerked open and Jericho stood glaring
down at me. A black curved-stem pipe was gripped be-

6

tween his strong white teeth. He was holding a palette in one hamlike hand and a brush in the other. Those huge hands could work with a concert pianist's dexterity when he was painting—and could punch a hole through a board fence when he was angry.

"Why don't you scram?" he asked coldly.

"I need help," I said, and walked past him into the brilliantly lighted room. A picture from his recent visit to Vietnam was on the easel. He'd obviously been trying to rework it.

"I'm not in a helping mood," Jericho said, and slammed the door shut, so hard that everything in the studio room shook. "You the one who's been calling me?"

I nodded. I was looking at the painting. "You fool around with that much more and you'll spoil it."

"I don't need help," he said.

He could have picked me up under one arm and thrown me out into the hall, but he didn't. He put his palette and brush down on the worktable beside the easel.

"Drink?" he asked, waving toward a side table.

The familiar bottle of bonded bourbon was there, ice in a wooden bucket, and a stack of limes in a bowl. Jericho has the foul habit of desecrating good bourbon by squeezing lime juice into it.

"You ever hear of Tommy Nolan?" I asked him, turning back to the Vietnam painting.

"You are an old enough friend to know that I don't want to be bugged with anything unimportant," he said. "If I wanted an excuse not to work, I'd have answered the

7

phone."

"Nolan committed suicide last night," I said.

"So it's too late to do anything for him," Jericho said. "Look, Hally, be a good fellow and buzz off."

I walked over to the side table and poured myself a short drink of bourbon on a couple of ice cubes. "You know his paintings, John?" I asked.

Jericho shrugged. "Not enough to form a solid judgment. The voice of today's youth. Isn't that his trademark? I'm not sure he makes me hear that voice."

"Would you recognize that voice if you heard it for real?" I asked.

"I've heard it," he said grimly. "I've heard it in the Vietnamese jungles and in the Saigon military hospitals. I've heard it, in another key, in draft-card-burning demonstrations and at campus riots. I don't know that in these confused times there is one clear voice of youth. So maybe Tommy Nolan was just whistling his own tune."

"A damned intriguing tune," I said.

Jericho sounded impatient. "You want a testimonial? You want a quote for a funeral oration?"

"I want you to help protect his memory from the vultures," I said.

His bright, restless eyes were suddenly focused steadily on me. "What vultures?" he asked.

"They nest behind chromium-trimmed desks on Madison Avenue," I said.

"Oh, come on, Hally! You know better than to—"

"Let me tell you how it is," I said. "I've never tried to

involve you in anything that didn't matter, have I?"

"Try to make it a very short story," he said, and turned to the bourbon bottle. . . .

It was a pretty short story at that stage of the proceedings. It began through a series of complete coincidences, as far as I'm concerned. If I hadn't been dining at The Players one night about six weeks before, and if Maury Zimmerman, chief salesman for TAB—Trans American Broadcasting to you—hadn't also been there, I'd have no story at all to tell.

Maury is a delightful little guy who sells millions of dollars' worth of television time to the big advertisers of the country. Maury stands about five feet two and is a very tough little elf. In the business they say that Maury's genius lies in selling the customer something he wants that Maury hasn't got to sell—and then finding it. In other words, he is a producer of the impossible. Some day, he freely admits, he won't be able to deliver what he promises and he will find himself collecting relief checks.

On the night that I got involved Maury was riding high. Helstrom Cosmetics had just bought the idea of doing an hour special on TAB. It was a $750,000 deal. A third of that was talent costs, and the star was to be Zelda Rankin, the girl singer who is pressing Barbra Streisand hard for the title "hottest property in television." The program was to be aimed directly at Youth with a capital Y, promoting a new line of beautifying creams, lotions, colognes, and what have you coming fresh on the market

9

from Helstrom Cosmetics.

Victor Helstrom, the genius-type president of the cosmetics company, had insisted on Zelda, who had an exclusive contract with another network. Maury had somehow wangled Zelda for TAB by trading off a TAB exclusive on one of the top comics.

Television as an industry is loaded with geniuses who collect their pay checks by talking earnestly about the "fresh and new" ideas they will promote and actually making sure they never do anything but copy successful ideas that have already been used. Barbra Streisand had done a special against the background of the Philadelphia Museum, so the geniuses at TAB decided that Zelda Rankin should also work against an art background. Maury, always on the ball, suggested Tommy Nolan, who was making a splurge as a young modern, a sort of voice-of-youth. Nolan, who'd been getting a lot of publicity but eating in the Automat, accepted much less than he should have to let his paintings be used as a background for Zelda. He didn't swallow the line and sinker along with the hook, however. He demanded and got the right to veto the specific way his paintings could be used. Maury sold his superiors on this, assuring them that Nolan was so delighted he could be conned into anything if there was any trouble.

The trouble they were bound to face, and which none of them mentioned, was an alcoholic queer named Perry Lewis who was married to Zelda Rankin and was her manager.

10

But to get back to that night at The Players. Maury joined me at the bar before dinner, and after a few scurrilous insults and half a martini something clicked in Maury's busy brain. He pointed a finger at me.

"Arthur Hallam, author of Kafkaesque novels, whose most recent book contained a much-quoted section on the John Held-flapper age of American youth."

"Guilty," I said.

He told me about Zelda and the cosmetics special. "I haven't noticed you on the best-seller list lately, Hally, so I assume you would not turn up your nose at ten G's and a week's exposure to one of the nation's glamour queens."

I got the story of the special. It was Maury's suggestion that I write a profile on Zelda Rankin. One of the top weeklies was willing, only it had to be done fast to hit the newsstands prior to the night of the TV special. I was ideal, Maury said, selling himself as he talked, because of my recent outburst on the youth of another generation. Before I could order a second drink, he'd gotten the magazine editor at home through an unlisted number, sewed up the deal, and I had an appointment with Zelda and her entourage for the next day.

Zelda and her husband and her boy friend and her lawyer and her P.R. man and her musical genius all have a positive place in this piece of violence, but they come on stage a little later. Suffice it to say that during my week of preparation I took Zelda to Tommy Nolan's studio to look at his paintings. I wanted her reactions—something quotable—on the work that was going to serve as a background for her show.

The result of that meeting was unexpected. Zelda, girl symbol of Youth, had no reaction. It was then I was certain she had no genuine connection with the youth of any age. Turn on the music and she caught fire. Turn it off and she had nothing to offer except a very beautiful and eager young body. Perhaps I shouldn't use the word "nothing." The point is, I was the one who reacted to Tommy Nolan's work. The minute I looked at it I knew I was in the presence of a modern Degas or Lautrec. There was humor; there was satiric brilliance, and there was a passionate espousal of a misunderstood generation. It was a cry, in vigorous line and color, for understanding and identity. It didn't deserve to be used as the background for an overheated girl singer. But I knew Nolan must need the money—just as I did.

I stayed on after Zelda headed elsewhere, having made certain that Nolan was not, at least on the spot, a potential bedfellow.

I found Nolan an attractive, stubborn, dedicated guy so full of the juices of life they almost scalded you. He had no use for me—having naturally tied me up with Zelda—until I mentioned my close friendship with Jericho. Jericho, it seemed, was one of the very few living painters young Mr. Nolan could even nod at. I promised to get him together with Jericho, but it never came about when he was alive.

I'd met my deadline—finished my profile of Zelda—

offered up a prayer for absolution, and gone back to the painful business of trying to get a new novel on the road when I got a telephone call one morning. I have an unlisted number, so it had to be a friend.

It was a stranger.

"You don't know me, Mr. Hallam," said a pleasant, husky, young girl's voice. "I'm Pat Barry."

"Pat for Patricia?" I asked.

"Patricia O'Hanlon Barry," she said. "I—I'm a friend of Tommy Nolan's."

That explained her a little. I'd given my private number to Nolan. "Welcome, friend," I said. Her voice made me feel a little younger and pleasantly flippant.

"Tommy is dead," she said. She sounded vague, as though she didn't believe what she was saying.

I couldn't take it in.

"Did you hear me, Mr. Hallam?"

"Yes," I said. "What happened? I saw him less than a week ago."

"The police say it was suicide," Pat Barry said. I could tell she didn't believe it.

"How?"

"Pills," she said.

"Was he a pill taker?"

"No. Mr. Hallam—?"

"Yes?"

"Can you come over to Tommy's studio? He wanted you to do something for him in case . . ."

"Then he did plan it?"

"Please. Can you come?"

"Half an hour," I said. . .

As a writer, I have invented a lot of girls. It's easy to describe the girls you invent. Patricia O'Hanlon Barry is something else again. The exteriors are easy enough. Blond, gold blond. Her hair was worn loose and down to her shoulders. It was expertly casual. That morning she was wearing tight-fitting slacks—the currently popular faded blue. They couldn't have been fitted off the rack. It was as if she'd been poured into them. The top was a black turtle-neck sweater that made very clear the magnificence of her upper proportions. Her mouth was wide and generous, with that very pale lipstick that looks like none at all. Her eyes were an incredible dark violet color. They were intense and yet suggested a bubbling humor lying behind them. That morning they were anxious. She had been wondering about me—and other things.

All this you could photograph in Panavision and it still wouldn't provide you with the extras, the difference between something that comes by the million in packages and something that comes just for once, with no mold that would make a repetition possible. There is, I think, a word in common use that describes it. Patricia O'Hanlon Barry was an original. One look at her and you were curious about a dozen things. How would she look dressed for the opera? How would she look with no clothes at all? How did she think? What would make her laugh? A girl with so

14

much going for her could be greedy, without compassion. Was it possible—and you instinctively prayed it wasn't— that this was all scenery painted over nothing—like Zelda Rankin?

Of course, that isn't fair to Zelda. With Zelda it's like drilling for oil and coming up with a first-class quality tap beer. It's a disappointment, but you can't knock the beer, and if you're a beer drinker, you might think of it as a ten-strike. And it isn't fair to Pat Barry, either. The first moment you lay eyes on her you want her to be all the things in the world you've ever wanted a woman to be. Who could match up to that?

Well, as I stood in the doorway of Tommy Nolan's studio and looked at Pat for my first time, I answered that question for myself. Pat could if any woman could.

I suppose a thousand men have looked at Pat the way I looked at her that first time—wondering, deep down inside hoping. And the damndest thing about it was that deep down hope involved more than just a personal dream. You hoped she would never disappoint you, whether you were the one or not. She had to be the girl of all time, or it would hurt.

At my age, a sophisticated novelist, I told myself I must be off my rocker. No strange golden girl could possibly matter that much. It occurred to me she was probably an empty-headed model who had posed for Tommy Nolan at a couple of bucks an hour.

"Please come in," she said.

Nolan's studio was just as it had been a few days ago—

15

pictures scattered around the walls. He'd been trying for long hours to select just the right ones to use in Zelda's special.

I'd bought a newspaper just before I took a cab across town. The story was front-page tabloid stuff. Nolan had been discovered by a cleaning woman who had a key to the place late the previous afternoon. He'd been sprawled out on the floor where he'd fallen and knocked his head against the corner of his worktable. The medical examiner's report indicated the blow on the head had been inconsequential. Nolan had taken on enough barbiturates to kill a horse. It wasn't an amount you could take by accident. He'd left no suicide note, called no friends. The police hadn't found a bottle or any kind of container in which the pills had been kept. The body had been naked. It was evident he'd gone to bed and gotten up later. His clothes were neatly hung over the back of a chair. It appeared he might have taken the pills, changed his mind as they began to take hold, staggered out into the studio to get to the phone, and fallen before he could reach it. There was a paragraph about the fact that his paintings were to be used in a TV special. It seemed he had spent the previous evening with Zelda Rankin, her husband, Perry Lewis, and Rich Ragsdale, who was to direct the program. Nolan, they all said, had been very much alive and apparently in perfect health when he left them shortly after midnight. There was no reason, they all said, for him to have been depressed. They were all delighted with his work. Things couldn't have been more harmonious. "A great loss to the younger generation of painters," Rich Ragsdale told the tabloid reporter. "A real doll," Zelda had said. "One of the really *in* people." His death, they all said, wouldn't alter the plan to use Nolan's work as the background for the special.

The incredible golden girl waited for me to say something. So I said, "Hello." And, "It still doesn't make very much sense to me."

"Tommy liked you," Pat said.

"You said there was something he wanted me to do."

"Please sit down," she said. "I've just made some fresh coffee. Have some?"

I said I would. I wanted to watch her walk across the room to the kitchenette. It wasn't a professional model's walk. She had on reasonably flat heels. She walked like someone who was used to swinging along a country road.

Her coffee was first-class and I told her so.

"A hundred per cent Colombian," she said. "Tommy buys it—used to buy it—in a special place on Third Avenue." She picked up her handbag from the mantel. From it she took a plain white envelope. "About a week ago Tommy gave me this," she said, and handed me the envelope.

I opened it and took out the sheet of paper it contained. It was dated ten days ago, typewritten. At the bottom was a notary's seal and the signature of two witnesses in addition to Nolan's. It said, with a little legal verbiage thrown in, that in the event anything should happen to him before the TAB special was complete, Miss Patricia O'Hanlon Barry was to have complete authority to act for him, if he was unable to act, or in his place if he should die. This was to supersede the authority of the artistic executor appointed in his will and to apply only to the TAB special.

"He seems to have been a young man who kept his affairs in order," I said.

"He believed passionately in the future of his work, Mr Hallam. He knew artists have a way of dying before they're recognized. He wanted to be prepared for that. His artistic executor is Dominick Estrada."

"One of the best moderns," I said.

"And in Spain for the next year," Pat said. "Tommy wanted his work shown on the special. It would be a big step forward in being recognized."

"He expected something to happen to him?" I asked, tapping the paper.

"No. He was just concerned about his work," Pat said. "Something could happen to him before the show. He could be run down by a taxi. Anything. He wanted to be sure the vultures didn't foul him up."

"Vultures?"

"The public-relations people for the broadcasting company; the public-relations people for the cosmetics people; the public-relations people for Zelda and her collection of bone pickers. You know what I mean?"

I knew what she meant.

"Tommy had veto power over what they did with his work," she said. "Now I have it."

"Fine," I said. "He's protected."

18

She shook her golden head. "I'm not an artist, Mr. Hallam. I don't know enough to protect him properly. He knew that, but he knew I'd find someone who'd tell me what to do if it was necessary. He had one person in mind."

"Oh?"

"Your friend, John Jericho," she said.

Nolan had certainly admired Jericho's work. He'd spoken of him like a disciple of the Master.

"Would Jericho take on the job?" she asked.

"He might," I said, thinking pretty certainly that he wouldn't.

"Don't play games with me, Mr. Hallam," she said, sharpness creeping into her voice.

"I can try to persuade him," I said. "You don't believe Tommy killed himself, do you?"

"How did you know?"

"I heard it in your voice on the phone. 'The police say . . .' you said."

"His work was good. His future was good. His sex life was good," she said quietly.

I felt a little twinge of regret. She couldn't be so sure of his sex life unless she was it. "His health?" I asked.

"His health was fine," she said.

"He had trouble sleeping?"

"Never."

"He didn't take pills to help him get to sleep?"

"Never."

"Then what was he doing with enough pills to provide

himself with a massive overdose?"

"He didn't have any pills."

"But the medical examiner—"

"I can't help that. He didn't have any pills."

"How can you be sure? Were you living with him?"

I regretted having asked it the instant it was out of my mouth. I was asking out of personal curiosity.

"If you are asking whether I hung my clothes in his closet, cooked his breakfast, ran his errands, the answer is no," she said coolly. "If you're asking whether I was in love with him, the answer is yes. If you're really asking how I know he didn't use pills, the answer is unreasonable. I know because I knew him. I know it because I knew him well enough so that if he'd had trouble sleeping he'd have told me. I was reasonably familiar with the medicine cabinet in his bathroom. He didn't need pills. He didn't take pills."

"So what happened?" I said.

"I'm not a policeman," she said, the violet eyes very bright. "I don't jump at easy ways out. I told them what I told you. One plain-clothesman—the bastard!—patted me softly on the behind and told me I was making a mountain out of a you-know-what. 'Where did he get the pills?' I asked him. 'You have to have a prescription for pills.' 'You have to,' he said, 'but that doesn't mean you can't get them without one. Did he patronize a particular drug-store?' I said he did and that the man there would assure him Tommy never took pills. 'Sure he will,' the cop said, 'particularly if Nolan was getting 'em without a prescrip-

20

tion.' After that this master mind asked me for dinner on his night off."

She was breathing as if she'd been running.

"How do they explain the absence of a bottle or pill-box?"

"Easily," Pat said. "He got the pills at the drugstore. He stopped somewhere for a drink—there was alcohol in his stomach and wherever else they could check it. He'd had a few drinks. Zelda's husband said he had liquor while he was with them. But the policeman chooses to think he stopped at a bar, swallowed his pills, and got rid of his bottle or box on the way home—long since disposed of by the Department of Sanitation. Easy as that!"

"So he came home, went to bed, and then when it was too late, tried to get to the phone for help?"

"That's it, and it's complete horse droppings," Pat said.

"What do you think happened?" I asked her. Nothing coming from her sounded vulgar or nasty. She was entirely natural and unself-conscious.

"You've just finished doing a research on Zelda and the upcoming piece of four-star garbage," Pat said. "What struck you most vividly about the whole setup, Mr. Hallam?"

It was when I tried to give her an honest answer to that question that I began to have a cold feeling along my spine. The word "murder" began to take shape in the back of my mind.

# Two

"So how did you answer her?" Jericho asked.

He was at the side table in his studio, pouring himself another lime-poisoned bourbon. I felt myself relaxing. I knew the story had hooked him.

"Will you look at Tommy Nolan's work?" I asked him.

He took a swallow of his drink. "And the girl," he said. He glanced at his wrist watch. "It's after midnight. Can it be done now?"

I knew it could. Pat Barry had told me that she was going to stay at Nolan's studio. She felt uneasy about leaving his paintings unguarded.

"Use your phone?" I asked Jericho.

Pat answered on the second ring. She sounded relieved when I told her Jericho was willing to come to the studio now.

It was a warm spring evening, with a moon high in the

sky above the darkened skyscrapers. New York is a pretty grubby, noisy, overpaced, intense place to live, but there is something about it on a spring night. The leaves on the few trees have not collected their summer's grime; the pavements are not yet scorching hot. The people you pass on the street look renewed, refreshed, and somehow a little younger. There is promise in the air. You know it's a promise that won't be kept, but you let yourself believe in it for a little stretch of time. For about five minutes, headed uptown in Jericho's red Mercedes convertible, I felt young and on the way to some sort of romantic adventure. He brought me sharply back to earth.

"You still haven't told me the answer you gave the girl about your most vivid impressions of the setup," he said. "I want to know what you told her."

The spring night began to turn a little sour.

I'd undertaken the job of doing the profile on Zelda with considerable interest. I'd never been on the inside of this business. I gathered that something over three quarters of a million dollars would be spent to put a slim, dark girl with an offbeat way of singing a song on forty million home screens for one hour. After that hour it would be forgotten, except for a possible rerun if it was a big success. Helstrom Cosmetics would be making a huge investment, gambling that it would pay off in hopped-up sales of lipsticks, face creams, bath oils, and shampoos. If it didn't pay off, heads would fall all along the line. Not Victor Helstrom's, even though he'd insisted on Zelda and okayed the deal. Maury Zimmerman, the salesman, would be a prime target. Rich Ragsdale, the director, would lose face. Al Stover, TAB's expert on specials and spectaculars, would be slowly roasted over the coals heated by all the second guessers in the tall buildings along Madison Avenue. And finally, Zelda herself could suffer a serious damage to her public image, her earning capacity, and her appeal to the huge teen-age audience that screamed and yelled at the very sight of her on the stage apron, just as they'd screamed and yelled at Sinatra twenty-odd years ago and the Beatles more recently. And for every prominent member of the team who might be tarnished by this one hour in time, a dozen smaller heads would be battered out of shape. It was, it seemed to me, like a gigantic game of roulette in which scores of players staked everything on one turn of the wheel.

But not really roulette, I told myself, because it wasn't all a matter of luck. There were big-time professionals on the job. *An Hour with Zelda Rankin* was not just an hour with Zelda and her special rhythms and phrasings of popular tunes. It was an hour also with Rich Ragsdale, who ranked at the top of the directorial heap along with Gower Champion and Mike Nichols. His name added to Zelda's made the show even bigger and more important. There was Zelda's accompanist and arranger, who invented her special rhythms and phrasings. There would be the brilliant and exciting paintings by Tommy Nolan. There were the shrewd manipulations by Al Stover, who had made the final decision that Zelda could carry an hour without special guests, which suggested she was in a class with Streisand and Lena Horne.

With props like these you couldn't call it roulette. They had a hell of a lot going for them, and I guessed the odds were long in favor of Victor Helstrom selling more cosmetics than he dreamed of on his most optimistic day.

And then as I began to dig into the details of this fascinating business gamble, my hair started to curl. This wasn't a cool, accomplished team working in skillful harmony together. This was a bag full of psychotic tiger cats, clawing and snarling and screaming at each other. People whose names you'd never see on the list of credits were at the center of a cockeyed power struggle, primarily Zelda's alcoholic husband, Perry Lewis. This young man's whims, daily changing, controlled each day's turmoil. He told Zelda what to do and what not to do. His name was on no contract, but he had the power to have his way because he controlled Zelda. When someone screamed "violation of contract" at Perry, he'd just smile, a sleepy, vicious smile, and say, "We don't refuse to do what you ask, but Zelda is sick. What can you do with a sick singer?"

One of the days I went to talk to Zelda about herself she appeared with Perry. She'd obviously been given a bad going over. Her cheekbone was bruised; one eye was swollen; her lip was cut.

"From time to time it becomes necessary," Perry told me, his eyes narrowed, his smile sardonic, "to make it quite clear who wears the pants in this family."

I started to protest when I saw Zelda's parted, trembling mouth, the almost hypnotized concentration on

Perry. She liked it! She didn't care that I was there. She was almost pleading for him to do it again.

I told Al Stover about it at lunch that day. The TAB expert looked old and tired, and the shooting was still weeks away. "When this show gets on the air, if it ever does," he said, "the picture will be clear and clean, the sound will be stereophonic, and Zelda's performance will be simple and magical. But those of us in the know will see only a murky fog of liquor and drugs and sex and murderous jealousies."

"I'm drooling for details," I said to Al.

"Better you shouldn't have them," he said, "or you'll never be able to write the piece we're paying you to write about Zelda. After the show is on tape and finished you may buy me ten or fifteen drinks, one right after the other, and I'll tell you what's what about each and every one of these babies. You may need help keeping your dinner down."

Jericho had pulled up outside the building where Tommy Nolan's studio was located. Looking down the deserted street, I could see a tugboat and barges moving down the East River, noiseless. Jericho made no move to get out of the car.

"I still want your answer to the girl's question," he said.

"I can't make it as simple for you as I did for her," I said, "because she already knew the answer. It involves a special world with its special climate. And I'm not trying to pun on the word 'special.'"

"Just assume that I'm slightly more than four years old,

Hally," Jericho said with exaggerated patience.

"Lawlessness is the key word, I guess," I said. I fished for a cigarette and lit it. "And I don't mean by that that the television business is run by crooks, although, curiously enough, I heard whispers about the involvement of 'the Syndicate,' whatever that means."

"I sometimes think 'the Syndicate' is every man's excuse for his own lack of conscience," Jericho said. " 'I did wrong, but there was a pistol at my back!' "

"It starts out with the money end of it," I said, trying once more to say it clearly. "It starts out with Zelda Rankin, a little girl from South Philadelphia, getting two hundred and fifty thousand dollars for appearing for one hour on television."

"You've caught the habit yourself," Jericho said. "It's two hundred and fifty thousand for the show, right? That includes Mr. Ragsdale, the musical geniuses, and dozens of others."

I nodded. "So Zelda's fee is about a hundred grand. But she can't afford to make it. Taxes. And so into the picture comes the world of accountants and dummy corporations and horse trading with other stars—a guest appearance for a guest appearance so that actually the outgo matches the intake. But what's important, Johnny, is the incredible inflation of individual importance. We've come out of the age where the big tycoon ran his business with an iron fist. The president of TAB, one of the four great broadcasting powers in the country, doesn't bang the top of his desk and tell Zelda Rankin to go jump in the lake. This is

27

the age of the star performer, Johnny. In a test of power the little girl from South Philadelphia can topple the head of a huge business. And the little girl from South Philadelphia is completely moral. She is for Zelda with a capital I. She will gratify her own psychotic needs with drugs, with a husband who beats her, with a lover who calmly steps into her bed each night after her husband passes out from too much hootch. She pushes each other piece on the board to the very edge of a cliff every day. And they push back. They all come to believe that none of the rules ever apply to them, and everyone else in the game knows that they don't. Their traffic tickets are fixed; the news media are fixed in terms of not exposing their private debaucheries and deviations; whatever they want can be gotten for them." I hesitated. "I probably still haven't made it clear, Johnny, but if they committed a murder for any reason whatsoever, it would be fixed for them."

"By whom?"

"By the system itself," I said. "The little girl from South Philadelphia and her private army of punks can get away with murder as long as she can attract forty million people to stay glued to their TV sets for an hour next month; for as long as the broadcasters can sell a half a million dollars' worth of air time on her name; for as long as she can sell a billion lipsticks for Victor Helstrom."

"And why would the little girl from South Philadelphia want to murder an artist who painted pictures of rebellious youth?" Jericho asked.

"Who knows?" I said. "Maybe she appeared before him

28

in a topless bathing suit and he wasn't impressed. More realistically, maybe he insisted on his pictures playing a more important part in this upcoming stupendosity than Zelda or Perry or Ragsdale wanted. So they decided to have it both ways. The punishment for being too big for his boots was death, but at the same time they'd still have the use of his name and his work. The key to this over-privileged society, Johnny, is that they have discovered how to beat the oldest game in the world. They have discovered how to have their cake and eat it too, every day in the week."

Jericho, his face rock-hard, looked up at the lighted third-story window of the brownstone before which we were parked. Down the river the tugboat hooted mournfully. From an open window up the block came the sweet-rough voice of Louis Armstrong over a banjo background turning "Hello, Dolly" into a jazz classic.

"Let's go meet the lady," Jericho said. . . .

. I don't like the women's fashions of the moment. I don't like the hem line above the knee. There aren't enough legs can take it. I don't like the shift that hangs from the shoulders like a nightgown, shapeless.

When Patricia O'Hanlon Barry opened the door of Nolan's studio, she was guilty of violating all my likes—and I felt myself breathing hard in spite of it. She wore a shift, a delicate yellow that somehow contrasted perfectly with the gold of her hair. The hem line was high. Her skin was tanned a lovely color so that I couldn't be certain or

29

not whether she was wearing stockings. She wasn't. She was wearing earrings, pendant style. The ear pieces and the little chains that supported what may or may not have been real lapis were of antique hammered silver. She was smoking a cigarette in a holder that matched the blue of the earrings.

In the background a stereo machine, turned very low, was playing something I was sure was Bartók.

She didn't even look at me. Her violet eyes were raised to Jericho. She had to look up at him. The top of her gold head scarcely reached his breastbone. For just an instant their eyes seemed to lock.

"I'm John Jericho," he said, his voice husky.

"I know," she said. "Please come in." Then she managed to look at me. "Thank you, Mr. Hallam."

"Be my guest," I said. She looked like a child—and yet not like a child. The electric currents that were passing between her and Jericho were not childish either.

It seemed to take an effort for my friend to walk past her into the studio room.

"Drink?" she asked from behind us. "I brought in a bottle of bourbon to keep me company."

"You're psychic," Jericho said. "You don't happen to have a lime, do you?"

"To put in the bourbon?"

He turned and grinned at her. "Yes, ma'am," he said.

"I'm sorry," she said.

"So am I," Jericho said. "Somehow I would expect you to anticipate everything." He turned quickly away, his

30

eyes narrowed in concentration on the dozens of pictures that were stacked around the room.

Tommy Nolan might be lying in an undertaker's establishment, but his work made a very lively impact. I realized that things were not just as they had been when I was last here. Pat Barry might not know anything about art, but she had arranged the paintings with a keen eye for making the best possible impression on Jericho. I saw him reach in his pocket for the black curved-stem pipe and fill it, like a man in a trance. Tommy Nolan had caught his complete attention. Suddenly he pointed his finger at a painting of a young girl, arms outstretched, reaching for something we couldn't see in the picture.

"How recent is that?" he asked Pat.

"The last thing he did," she said quietly.

"The man who painted that wasn't suicidal," Jericho said, his voice harsh. "It's full of life and dreams and blazing hope." He turned to Pat. "Exactly what is it you want me to do?"

"Now that he's not here, to make sure they don't sell him out on this show," she said.

"Why should they sell him out?" he asked.

"Why should they kill him?" she countered.

"That's wild talk," he said impatiently. "You loved the guy, so you don't want to admit that anything went sour for him."

"I didn't love him," she said, quite steadily, "and I don't believe anything went sour for him—not suicidally sour."

So she hadn't loved Tommy Nolan, but he had been her

31

lover. I saw Jericho had the same thought and I wondered if it disappointed him as it disappointed me. Or was I just old fuddy-duddy Hallam who didn't understand the mores of another generation?

"You found him?" Jericho asked quietly.

"Yes."

"Here in this room?"

"The police drew chalk marks on the floor there by the worktable," she said. "I scrubbed them out when they were through. I—I have a key to the place. I found him. He was stark naked, poor darling. His head was all bloodied. I covered him up with the bedspread. I knew how he'd hate being seen that way by the police."

"You called them?"

"It's the law, isn't it?"

Jericho held a lighter to the bowl of his pipe, puffing acrid blue smoke into the atmosphere. "You're asking me to do two things for you, Pat," he said.

"Yes."

He stared at the portrait of the girl, reaching with such passionate hope for something beyond her. She'd asked him to protect the interests of the dead artist with the TV people.

"They wanted him to repaint that picture," Pat said, with an edge of bitterness, "with Zelda Rankin's face! The camera would come in close on the picture and then the film would dissolve to the real Zelda."

"Oh God!" Jericho said. "He refused, of course?"

"Of course. He went to Zelda's apartment last night to

tell them exactly where they could stuff that idea. Now that he's gone, they'll probably get some cartoonist to—"

"The hell they will," Jericho said.

"Thank you," Pat said quietly.

"But I will not play private detective," Jericho said.

"Tommy was murdered," she said.

"So persuade the police!" Jericho thundered at her. "So look in the Yellow Pages for a private eye. The directory is full of 'em."

"He deserves the best," she said.

"I'm not a cop!" Jericho said.

"I know all about you," she said. "You're in the door, Jericho. You're the guardian of Tommy's work as far as this TV thing is concerned. In five minutes you'll know whether I'm dreaming or not."

"Flattery'll get you no place," Jericho said, staring hard at the painting of the reaching girl.

"I'm not trying to flatter you," she said. His shouting didn't bother her. "When you meet this Rankin crew, you'll make up your own mind and it won't matter whether I've asked you or not."

"Don't count on it!"

Her smile was as wise as all Time. She didn't say anything.

"How badly did he need the money—for letting them use his work?" Jericho asked.

"Badly."

"He doesn't need it now. We can tell them to go fry themselves."

"A legal contract was signed," Pat said. "They can use the work. The only control we have is over how they use it."

Jericho's smile was grim. "Then we can make it damned difficult for them," he said.

"I'd like that," Pat said.

Jericho glanced at his watch and then at me. "Where are these people at two in the morning?"

"Maybe on the town," I said. "Maybe whooping it up at home. At two A.M. Perry Lewis has just about lost interest in the proceedings and Master Donald Ferrick will have taken over Zelda for the rest of the night."

"Ferrick's the boy friend?"

"Among other things."

"Meaning?"

"He has to be seen to be believed," I said. "Almost as big as you. Long hair, coifed around his face and over his ears like a woman's. Pinch-waisted, padded-shoulder, double-breasted jackets with wide side vents. He models the ultra newest fashions for the way-in crowd. He makes a point of being seen in the sharpest night spots in his pale-green or canary-yellow polka-dot dinner jacket, with lace cuffs, and a lace-frilled dress shirt, tight pants. And if anyone suggests out loud that he may be a little queer, he breaks them in half. He used to be a professional athlete and stunt man in Hollywood."

"I've made a note," Jericho said. He turned to Pat. "You say Tommy Nolan went to see the Rankin entourage last night to have it out with them about changing that painting into a likeness of Zelda?"

"Among other things. I saw him just before he left."
Pat's eyes clouded. "He suggested I go with him. I refused. I wish I hadn't."

"All he had to do was say 'No,' wasn't it? Why did he
have to go to see them?"

"They have a special technique," Pat said. "Everybody
in the business has it—network people, advertisers, as
well as the talent. They never listen to a 'No.' The theory
is you can be worn down. Tommy said 'No' to that pro-
posed likeness of Zelda over two weeks ago. Yet every day
it would come up again, as though it hadn't been mentioned before, or as though it had been agreed to. In the
end Tommy was supposed to throw up his hands and
agree. Last night Ragsdale, the director, called to talk
about certain effects he thought would be good. In the
process he mentioned the likeness of Zelda as though it
were a settled thing. Tommy didn't throw in the towel,
but he blew his stack. He gathered from Ragsdale they
were all at Zelda's, including Al Stover, the TAB special
man. He decided he'd go and say 'No' to all of them once
and for all."

"You didn't see him afterward?"

"No. I expected him to call me at my apartment when
he got home to tell me how it came out. He didn't. I called
him here about three in the morning, but he didn't answer. I guessed he'd gotten himself into an all-night
wrangle, so I went to sleep. Next morning I was curious,
so I decided to come over and make his breakfast for him

35

and be brought up to date. I—I found him, there on the floor."

Jericho stared for a long time at the paintings. "I think I'd like to find out about that all-night wrangle," he said. He turned to me. "Where do I find them, Hally?"

# Three

Zelda Rankovitz grew up in extreme poverty. She was one of eleven kids. Her old man was a longshoreman on the Philadelphia docks, immersed all his life in violence and backbreaking hard labor. Her mother had been a burlesque stripper who got incautious enough one night to go over to Camden with Steve Rankovitz and marry him. She then had eleven kids in the space of thirteen years. She was a scrawny, drunken, bitter wreck of a woman about the time that a crate of farm machinery broke loose from a crane on Pier X and landed on Steve Rankovitz' back, leaving him a helpless cripple. The insurance provided less than enough to take care of Steve's medical care, let alone his enormous family. Some of the kids turned to legitimate work; some of the boys got into the rackets, and Zelda won an amateur contest at a local movie house. The prize was a basket of groceries and the chance to compete in some sort of final contest in a bigger movie house.

It was one of those miracles. Someone heard her and gave her a chance to sing in one of the new a-go-go places springing up around town. Someone else heard her there and gave her a chance to make a record. In less than a year Zelda, her name shortened to Rankin, was making a lot of money. Her father was taken to a modestly expensive nursing home where he died before he could get to enjoy the better care. Her mother, relieved of the burdens of physical labor, managed to drink herself to death in an incredibly short space of time.

Zelda was alone then, her obligations, if they'd ever really existed, fulfilled. She made a half million dollars the next year and she was suddenly surrounded by the new mob who were to feed off her forever.

Perry Lewis, a clarinet player in a jazz combo, got there first, dark, intense, and wildly psychotic. He had been born with a crippled foot, and his bitterness over this misfortune was aimed at everyone who came within range of his caustic tongue and his sadistic techniques. I'm not a psychiatrist, but I gather that Zelda's masochistic tendencies made them a perfect match. And Zelda's enormous earning power and her quickly achieved position at the pinnacle of show business allowed them to indulge themselves in anything in the world they wanted.

One of these indulgences was the purchase of three adjoining brownstone houses in New York's East Sixties. The house on the east end was turned into a business office for

Zelda's multiplying ventures and an upstairs living setup for Perry when they were mad at each other. The house on the other end was where they lived when they were speaking to each other and where Zelda lived when they weren't. The house in the center was where they raised hell!

It was a museum of pop art. It had a huge music room that took up one whole floor with piano, pipe organ, and a bar that ran one long length of the room. Upstairs were what Perry called their "orgy rooms." God alone knows what went on there. They could raise an endless din in that center house and there was no one to complain, because they owned the adjoining houses. They were, by the very nature of Zelda's work, night people. Their fun time started when almost everyone else had gone to bed. They had never heard of a quiet evening at home.

I mention all this because there are thousands of people who will spring to Zelda's defense, justifying the extremes of her private life on the almost unendurable childhood. Maybe she's entitled to that defense. And she had a way with a song, God knows. She might not be my dish of tea or yours, but her bank account proved she had a way. I also mention all this to explain why I had no qualms about taking Jericho to the Hell Hole, which is what Perry Lewis called the center house, at half-past two in the morning. You didn't have to call Perry and Zelda to find out if they were up.

I was in part prepared for what we ran into at the Hell Hole. I'd spent a couple of evenings there during the writing of my piece on Zelda. She was doing two shows a night at one of the most popular discotheques. After the second show she and her mob, along with whoever else might have been collected during the night, would repair to the Hell Hole. It would start out like a fairly normal evening. Jimmy Cooper, who was Zelda's accompanist, would plunk himself down at the piano. He was a round, bald little man with a perpetual cigar stub in one corner of his mouth. He could make a piano sit up and say uncle. I think he knows every jazz tune and show tune that's ever been written. He goes back to old-time New Orleans Dixieland and carries right through to the newest Beatle chant. He's not frilly. He's solid and full—so full that he sounds like two people playing—and he has a left-hand beat that shakes the building. He can make even me want to dance, to move. Zelda really likes to sing. She doesn't save herself for her public. She and Jimmy can go on for hours if the mood is on.

"I used to play the piano in a fancy cat house in Chicago," Jimmy said. "The management offered fifty bucks to anyone who could stump the piano player. I had to know everything, because if I was stumped, the fifty bucks came out of my pay."

Perry Lewis drinks steadily but in a controlled fashion all evening until he gets home. Then he really pours it on. He gets behind that long bar, sets them up for the guests, and he has one for himself with every one he makes for someone else. Once in a while the music mood hits him and he takes his black licorice stick out from behind the

40

bar and joins in for a phrase or two. I've heard him play
five or six bars that would make Benny Goodman look up.
But only once or twice an evening. Finally, after an hour
or so, he pours a whole bottle of scotch over shaved ice
into a wide-mouthed thermos jug and lies down on a low
divan in a far corner of the room. He watches the proceedings out of narrowed, bloodshot eyes, and when the
thermos is empty, he goes to sleep. It is then that Don
Ferrick seems to materialize out of nowhere, incredible in
his Mod wardrobe and his long hairdo, and takes charge
of Zelda. You can see her eyes go animal bright and the
color mount in her cheeks. Jimmy Cooper never lets up at
the piano. There'll come a moment when he goes into
something really spectacular that makes you focus on
him. When it's over and everyone's shouting and applaud-
ing, you suddenly realize that Zelda and Don Ferrick have
disappeared for the evening. The party goes on as long as
anyone wants to drink and listen to Jimmy, but the host is
out cold and the hostess has gone on to bigger and better
things.

Jericho should have been prepared by what I told him,
he admitted to me later, but he wasn't. The street seemed
quiet enough. There were no visible lights in the center
house of the three brownstones. Jericho imagined, when I
rang the doorbell, that we were about to discover that
Perry and Zelda were having a night out on the town. But
the front door was opened for us presently by Marty
Farmer. Marty is Zelda's public relations boy, and I'd had
quite a little contact with him during my piece writing.

41

"Hi, Maestro," he said to me, and looked curiously at the giant red-bearded man beside me.

I introduced them with identifying explanations for each of them. "Is anybody sober enough to make any sense?" I asked Marty.

"It depends on what you want to make sense about, Hally," Marty said. "You know how it is. We can always make sense if we want to, and not if not."

Jericho's eyes were raised toward the ceiling. There was the muffled sound of the piano and a kind of heavy, rhythmic stamping of feet. And above it all were the high, wavering notes of a clarinet.

"My friend Jericho has been put in charge of Tommy Nolan's paintings," I said. "He thought he ought to get straightened away as quickly as possible with Perry and Zelda and Rich Ragsdale."

Marty Farmer, on the surface, is permanently involved with laughter. I daresay his own mother has never penetrated that façade to know what goes on inside him. He's short and dark with bright black eyes that are never still.

"You have created a coincidence," he said to me. "At this very moment, upstairs, they are holding a wake for Tommy Nolan."

"A wake?" Jericho's voice was sharp.

"The poor lad had no one else to grieve for him—or so they tell me," Marty said. "Come on up and join the caterwauling."

We started up the thickly carpeted stair to the second floor. The music was clearer now. Jimmy Cooper was pounding out the theme song from the Beatles' movie *Help!* Above the piano came the high, piercingly clear sound of Zelda's voice:

*"Oh, won't you he-e-elp me!"*

It was echoed by the high wail of Perry's clarinet. Evidently he was still on his feet.

We walked across the threshold into the big music room and stood there, riveted.

In the center of the room a painting of Tommy Nolan's stood on a high-backed chair. There were flowers on the chair and on the floor around the chair. They looked like flowers that had been taken out of vases in the house. The stems were shiny wet. There were three corsages in the lot.

Bald Jimmy Cooper bobbed his cigar at us and went on pounding out the *Help!* theme. Zelda stood beside him, a hand on his shoulder, singing. Around the chair moved a column of people, dancing and singing. They were led by a limping Pannish figure playing his black flute—Perry and his clarinet. Others in the line were Rich Ragsdale, the director, Don Ferrick, a couple of gals in the new transparent evening gowns that leave practically nothing to the imagination, a man whom I recognized as Mike Crowley, the public relations man for Helstrom Cosmetics, and, of all people, Al Stover, TAB's expert on the TV special. There was an attractive girl hanging onto Al from behind who looked as if she wished she wasn't there. And there were two long-haired young men in Don Ferrick's special brand of tight pants and polka-dot dinner jackets.

They might be the seminude young women's escorts. They danced and pranced and shouted the *Help!* tune.

Before I knew what he was up to, Jericho walked to the chair, picked up the picture, tucked it under his arm, and walked toward the door with it.

Jimmy Cooper's piano stopped on a discord. Before Jericho reached the door, Don Ferrick, moving quickly, was barring his way. They were strange-looking antagonists. The room, which had been throbbing with noise, was suddenly deadly still.

"Put it back," Ferrick said in a quiet, level voice. There was the faintest of British intonations. He stood gracefully balanced on the balls of his feet. He looked out of another age with his ruffled shirt front and cuffs, the orange and black polka-dot dinner jacket with its wide side vents, the tight-fitting black trousers with an orange satin stripe down each side seam. The long hair cascaded down over the extreme high collar. He was an Edwardian dandy. You half expected the snuffbox to appear.

I was standing where I could see his eyes. They looked like pale amber ice cubes.

Jericho wasn't more than an inch taller. He looked somehow crude in his loose-fitting brown tweed jacket, gray slacks, navy-blue sports shirt with a turtle-neck collar. The dandy and the clod.

"Put it back," Ferrick said again. "Exactly where you got it."

One of the seminude girls giggled hysterically.

Jericho's voice was cheerful, conversational. "I am act-

44

ing for the legal custodian of Tommy Nolan's paintings," he said. "We don't like the use to which this picture is being put."

"That painting belongs to Perry," Ferrick said. "He bought it from Nolan about a month ago. It doesn't belong to Nolan or his estate any more. So put it back."

"The work of any important artist doesn't belong to an owner—it belongs to the ages," Jericho said, smiling a thin smile. "Your friend"—and he nodded toward an ash-pale Perry Lewis—"has only bought the right to act as the painting's guardian. This drunken obscenity forfeits him his rights to the picture. See you around, Buster."

Ferrick's left hand went out and the tips of his strong, square fingers tapped on Jericho's chest. "Put it back," he said. His voice was suddenly a low, excited whisper. "I warn you, big as you are, you will regret very much not doing what you're told."

Jericho had the painting tucked under his left arm. I had the uncomfortable feeling I hadn't impressed him properly with Ferrick's background as a professional athlete and stunt man. There were some pretty bad stories about his exploits around town. Some people had been severely hurt, and only Zelda's money and the persuasion of the people who wanted Zelda to remain a money-making machine for them had kept Ferrick from a series of homicidal assault charges. They said that he seemed to go completely out of control when his cork was pulled. I sensed, from the trembling whisper of his voice, that we were about to see a sample.

45

We didn't.

Jericho, eyeball to eyeball with this curious dandy, raised his right foot and brought his brass-cleated leather heel down viciously on Ferrick's black-patent-leather instep. Ferrick doubled forward with an involuntary cry of pain. The edge of Jericho's huge right hand came down on the back of Ferrick's neck in a chopping blow.

Ferrick sprawled on the floor, motionless.

I heard a trembling sigh from the girl giggler.

"Hang onto this for a minute, will you, Hally?" Jericho asked, passing me the painting.

Then he bent down and picked up the unconscious Don Ferrick as though he were a small child. He carried him over to the chair in the center of the room and put him, face-down, on the seat of it. Then he picked up an armful of flowers and tossed them over the still figure.

"A wake's no fun without a body," he said, grinning at the circle of frozen faces. "Carry on, kids. And when any of you want to talk seriously about the use of Tommy Nolan's paintings in your television opera, let me know." He came back to me. "Thanks, chum," he said, and took back the painting.

We started down the stairs. No one had spoken. My back ached in anticipation of some sort of attack from the rear, but it didn't come. Just as we reached the front door, somebody upstairs started to laugh. It was a wild sort of hysterical laughter, uncontrollable. I could have sworn it was Perry Lewis.

46

The piano jumped to life. Jimmy Cooper was jazzing up "Good Night, Sweetheart, 'Till We Meet Tomorrow."

When the front door closed behind us, the Hell Hole was shut away from the city as though it didn't exist.

"Forgive the fireworks," Jericho said.

Flamboyance is a part of his existence, but I know him well enough to know he hadn't put on that show simply to impress.

"Our fancy-pants friend is a tough cookie," I said. "I have the feeling you'll hear from him again."

"I count on it," Jericho said.

We started walking down the block to where the Mercedes was parked. Jericho was scowling. "Don't ask me why," he said, "but I have a solid feeling that your Miss Barry is right."

"*My* Miss Barry?"

He grinned at me. "You look at her like a lovesick spaniel, Hally."

"She left you untouched?" I asked.

"That one leaves no one untouched," he said. He stopped by the red car and put the painting carefully on the back seat and then turned to look at me. "I ought to give you a good solid boot in the behind," he said.

"Why?"

"You faked me into this, friend, with all that talk about my artistic integrity and the need to protect Nolan from the Madison Avenue vultures. You were convinced someone killed Tommy Nolan and wanted to convince me."

"So?"

"So I'm convinced. God knows how many days' work will be lost."

"Forget it then," I said.

"The boy could paint," Jericho muttered.

"You're not obligated to do anything about it," I said.

"You were right about those creeps back there," he said. "Have their cake and eat it."

"They're not your responsibility," I said.

"Nolan had something to say. They shut him up. Why? Are they so far gone they'd kill him just because he refused to draw a cartoon of Zelda for them?"

"What did you think of Zelda?"

"I hardly looked at her," he said.

"She's the queen bee," I said. "Everything revolves around her."

"I should never have let you into my studio tonight," he said. He hunched his big shoulders. "I'm hungry. Zirato's stays open all night, doesn't it? Let's go."

Just as he reached for the car door, someone hailed me from the direction of the brownstones. It was Al Stover. The TAB man had his nice-looking girl friend with him. They hurried along the sidewalk to us.

"Brother!" Al said. He was sweating. "This is my secretary, Miss Heller."

She was dark, with rather spectacular blue eyes. The way she clung to Al, I suspected she did something a little more for him than take dictation.

"You're John Jericho, aren't you?" Al said to my friend. "Quite a moment back there."

"Are they dancing around him?" Jericho asked.

"Believe it or not, yes. With Perry blowing a particularly bright tune on his clarinet. He seems to have enjoyed it all."

"Glad I pleased someone," Jericho said.

"I need to talk to you both," Al said. "Can we go somewhere?"

"I'm headed for a breakfast steak at Zirato's. Join us," Jericho suggested.

He moved the picture off the back seat of the car without waiting for an answer. He assumed it. He opened the door for Miss Heller.

"I can't tell you how glad I am to get away from there," she said with a little shudder.

Al got into the back seat with her. I sat in front with Jericho, holding the Nolan painting in my lap. I glanced up into the rearview mirror. Miss Heller had snuggled close to Al, her arm locked through his. He looked like death, I thought. Normally he's a nice-looking, relaxed guy who gives out an aura of complete competence at his job. Tonight he looked beaten to the edge of collapse.

"This particular job a little wearing?" I asked him.

I saw him lift his free hand and cover his eyes with it. "You can laugh about it before and after, but when you're in the middle, it's just plain, unadulterated hell."

"Which one of them killed Tommy Nolan?" Jericho asked casually, as he turned the Mercedes down Second

49

Avenue.

I saw Al's hand jerk away from his eyes, saw him stare at the back of Jericho's head. Miss Heller reached up to his cheek with the tips of her fingers. Then her eyes met mine in the mirror and she quickly pulled her hand away from Al's face.

Al gave a mirthless little laugh. "I almost thought you meant it for a moment," he said. "In a way I suppose you could say they did kill him."

"I do say it," Jericho said cheerfully.

"I've been in this business twenty years," Al said. "I've had to con my way with all the top crackpots on record. The Zelda Rankin complex tops 'em all. It could drive an unprepared guy off his rocker. So I suppose you could say they drove Nolan to suicide."

"I don't say that," Jericho said. "I say someone slipped him a Mickey and he died of it."

"You're kidding," Al said. I saw him moisten his lips. Miss Heller's face was a pale mask. She knew I was watching her now, and she kept her eyes lowered.

"Never more serious in my life," Jericho said. "Let's save it till we get settled in Zirato's."

I was surprised at the reactions of my friends in the back seat for a moment. I wondered why they should seem to be so stunned by Jericho's offhand suggestion. And then I realized that there was one area where a fellow in Al's position couldn't take anything lightly. It was his job to wet-nurse the Zelda Rankin show into being. If he failed, for whatever reason, his head was on the chopping block for his boss to hack off and hand to *his* boss as the excuse for failure.

"How soon are you supposed to start shooting the special, Al?" I asked.

"Monday—three days," Al said, as if he'd only half heard. "Old Parthenon Studios out in Brooklyn. You think everything is all honey and almond cream, ready to go? Night before this last one I spent with those creeps, trying to talk young Nolan into something he absolutely says he won't do. I'm the mediator, you understand, the man in the middle. All day I spend with the unions, trying to talk them out of technicalities that will add sixty thousand dollars to our costs. Back tonight with the creeps to figure out what we'll really do about Nolan's stuff, and guess at whether his suicide will help or hurt us. And do you think we can talk? I bring Lillian here along to take notes. You know what she's got? A comic funeral oration by Perry, four drinks she didn't want, and that snake dance to the Beatle anthem!"

"And you, Mr. Jericho," Lillian Heller said. She laughed. "Like a very fine, fresh wind out of nowhere."

"I aim to please," Jericho said.

Al looked worried again. "Ferrick might forgive your beating him to the draw, Jericho, but he'll never forgive your making him look foolish by draping him over that chair and dropping flowers on him. He'll find a way to get even if it takes him months."

"My blood runneth cold," Jericho said dryly.

Al leaned forward to make sure Jericho heard him.

"Ferrick is a crippler," he said. "I know one guy who hasn't been out of a wheel chair since he crossed Ferrick. Another is walking around with a black patch over an eye that isn't there."

"How does he get away with it?" Jericho asked.

"No proof in these two cases—stab in the back, you might say. His lesser run-ins he pays for, or rather Zelda pays for. I was asked two questions when the network agreed to go along with a Zelda special. Could I keep Perry in line, and could I keep Ferrick in line?"

Jericho chuckled. "And you said you could, so I'm safe!"

"I wish to God I could promise it," Al said, and sat back in his seat, his eyes closed wearily. I saw Lillian Heller rest her cheek against his shoulder. Al had a young lady there who was really in love with him.

Jericho found a place to park about a block from Zirato's. We all walked down the sidewalk to the restaurant, I carrying the Nolan painting.

Bernie Zirato, the owner of this particular saloon, is an old friend of Jericho's. How Jericho pulled Bernie's chestnuts out of an underworld fire is a story to be told somewhere else. The fact remains that Bernie would lie down and let the Second Avenue traffic run over him if Jericho asked it. Bernie is a square bear of a man. He beat and pounded at Jericho with delight when he saw him. There was no table available when we arrived, but seconds later one appeared out of nowhere and was set up close to the bar.

"A double bourbon on the rocks with lime juice for you, Johnny," Bernie said. "And for your friends—?"

I elected a stinger. Al took scotch and soda. Lillian said she really didn't want a drink and allowed Bernie to talk her into a brandy Alexander.

Zirato's place has its own special personality. I don't know who dreamed up the décor for Bernie, but the heavy beams and the red brick walls and floor suggested a Norman influence. Bernie was about as British in his background as Chico Marx. Its reputation was based on the massive sandwich, hot or cold, round the clock, and great wooden bowls of mixed green salad with Bernie's own special Italian garlic dressing or a pungent Gorgonzola cheese mixture. The bread was served in loaves, pumpernickel or Italian, on a board with a sharp knife. You did your own cutting, thick or thin. The liquor was measured in two-ounce shot glasses, and then a little extra slug from the bottle was added if you were a friend. Bernie was unique in one respect. There was no television and no jukebox. It was a place to talk. Not quietly, you understand. Bernie's customers shouted happily at each other, argued, threatened, and laughed and laughed. You were supposed to have a good time at Bernie's, and if anybody got sour or tough, four mammoth waiters appeared and deposited the offender out on his can on the sidewalk.

"This is a lovely place," Lillian said, her blue eyes wide. "I never saw anything like it."

"You want to make a speech?" Jericho asked.

Lillian looked startled.

"You go over to the bar and beat that big brass gong. They call it the Arthur Rank Special. You are then entitled to thirty uninterrupted seconds of oratory. Want to try?"

"Oh my, no!" Lillian said, laughing.

A waiter took our order. Lillian and Al Stover didn't seem to be very hungry. Jericho ordered a platter of antipasto to be shared between them. He asked for the extra-large steak sandwich for himself, with sliced raw Bermuda onion and a fried green tomato. I went for a slab of hot corned beef on rye. I felt better already. Al Stover looked like a man with an ulcer.

"I take it that Patricia O'Hanlon Barry has asked you to act for her on behalf of Nolan's paintings," he said to Jericho.

"And on behalf of Nolan," Jericho said, sipping his limed-up bourbon.

"Are you going to make trouble for us, just for the hell of it?" Al asked, without rancor.

"As far as Nolan's paintings are concerned, Al, I don't expect to be too hard to deal with. I take it that aging crewcut gent back at the wake was Ragsdale?"

"He's very big in our business," Al said. "His name on the masthead will draw just about as many people to their TV sets as Zelda's."

"It was his idea that Nolan should satirize a very beautiful and moving painting by substituting Zelda's face?"

"It was an idea," Al said. "If Nolan had said yes, with-

54

out making a fuss, Rich would probably have changed his mind. In the long run he has pretty good taste. But then when Nolan said 'No,' loud and clear, Rich got stubborn. He doesn't like anyone to say 'No' to him. My suggestion is that you don't mention it, and he won't try to use it."

"You can pass the word along to your higher-ups that if Ragsdale tries to do it, or anything else I don't like, they'll be sued for the entire west side of Madison Avenue," Jericho said cheerfully. "I'm not going to tell Mr. Ragsdale how to use the paintings in his show. Only how not to use them if he makes me unhappy." Bright blue eyes fixed steadily on Al over the rim of his glass. "Tell me about last night—Nolan's last night."

Al closed his eyes for a moment. The circles under them were dark and puffy. "It was like a thousand other nights," he said wearily. "The hours are creeping by on us. We're supposed to go before the cameras on Monday. Some things are settled. What Zelda will sing is settled. There are some numbers in which only Jimmy Cooper will play the piano behind her. There are some numbers that will add some percussion and a trumpet to Jimmy. The musicians will not be seen on the show. Only Zelda. This is the lament of modern youth, the protest of modern youth, the dream of modern youth. In the very beginning they thought of dancers behind her, elaborate choreography. Victor Helstrom didn't like the idea. He wants to sell cosmetics to teen-agers, but he doesn't like teen-agers. They are, he tells us, gross! Someone suggests he get Nelson Eddy to do a show that bears no relation to teen-agers.

Victor is annoyed by this. It was Ragsdale who came up with the brilliant idea of Nolan's paintings. These aren't a bunch of pansy dancers and bosomy dames exhibiting fancy footwork. These paintings *are* the laments, the protests, the dreams of modern youth. The kids watching, Ragsdale thinks, will go wild for them. Zelda, in her way, conveys a message. The paintings convey a message. Together, the impact should be terrific. When Nolan agreed, we figured we were in with something that wouldn't be forgotten for a long, long time. We left it to Rich Ragsdale to figure out how he'd use the pictures. The rest of us, from Victor Helstrom on down to me, to coin a phrase, were very, very happy."

"What went wrong?" Jericho asked.

"Nolan and Ragsdale went wrong. Ragsdale went to Nolan's studio to look at pictures and discuss with him how they could be most effectively used. You have to give Rich this much. The paintings really swept him off his feet. His enthusiasm for them was genuine and boundless. The picture that knocked him over was the one of the girl reaching out into space. He offered to buy it. Nolan could name his own price. Nolan wouldn't sell. I think he tried, in a clumsy sort of way, to explain. He didn't want it to go away from him yet. I suppose you can say it was an experience he was still having. Rich didn't get it. He convinced himself that Nolan was saying he didn't want Rich to own the picture. From that moment on he hated Nolan's guts. He's grown old in the last month, torn between his desire to hurt Nolan and his genuine admiration for the paintings and his conviction that he's going to be able to create a memorable show around them. He came up with the silly idea of painting Zelda's face into a striking picture. He would have been contemptuous of Nolan if he'd agreed, but he was also angry at him for having the guts to say 'No' to the great Ragsdale. Everybody got into the act trying to persuade Nolan—Zelda, Perry, Marty Farmer, Crowley—who's Helstrom's man—Don Ferrick, me—the whole team. Nolan said 'No' till he was hoarse. Then last night Rich called him about something and mentioned the change of the painting—putting Zelda's face in—as though it had all been agreed. Nolan blew his top and came charging over to the Hell Hole like a runaway fire truck. I was there. Everybody was a little tight as always. Nolan shouted and yelled and screamed at us—and had a few drinks. It was all adding up to nothing—a series of drunken ultimatums and counter ultimatums. I saw it wasn't going anywhere and I sat down in a corner with Mike Crowley and Marty Farmer to discuss promotion ideas. The time was coming for things to get moving. Maybe we talked together for forty-five minutes. When I turned back to join the main fight, I saw that Nolan was a little tight. First time I'd ever seen him that way."

"Who was the bartender?" Jericho asked.

"Perry, as always. But that doesn't mean you can't go behind and make your own drink. Perry was filling that big thermos jug with shaved ice and scotch, which meant he was about to withdraw to his divan and pass out. Rich was sitting cross-legged on the floor, a sort of Noel Cow-

57

ard Buddha. Nolan walked over to him and shouted at him: 'No! *No! NO!*' Then he turned, a little unsteady, and marched out the door and down the stairs to the street. That's the last I ever saw him."

"You think he went from there to buy some pills and knock himself off?" Jericho asked.

"It's hard to believe," Al said. "He was a very alive kid, full of fight, full of plans. But he must have."

"I say he couldn't have," Jericho said placidly. The waiter had arrived with his two-pound steak sandwich.

There was a pause while the table was loaded with food, while our drinks were replenished on the house, while Bernie stood by, rubbing his hands together and hoping we were simply delighted with everything.

"You have to catch on to the point of view, Jericho," Al said earnestly, as soon as the waiters and Bernie had evaporated. He showed no interest in a mouth-watering platter of antipasto. "We live in a vicious world. I mean those of us who are in the overblown areas of show business. Everything is out of balance. When a little girl from the Philadelphia-Camden docks can make X millions of dollars a year while an atomic scientist, who holds our lives in his hands, is drawing seven thousand a year at some Midwestern college, things are out of balance. Show business, particularly the TV aspects of it, is a jungle. A big star can go from the very top of the heap to the third subcellar so fast you can't recognize him as he whizzes past. With the greased skids yawning all around you, you

58

don't bother with the Marquis of Queensberry rules. You cut throats, you lie, you cheat, you steal, you evade, you equivocate, you damage the competition in any way you can. It's murder, but not murder the way you mean it, Jericho. Anyone back there at the Hell Hole would destroy your career, your reputation, your chances of a future without thinking twice. But to murder Tommy Nolan just because he wouldn't agree to having one of his paintings used in a cheap way—its just simple nonsense. Not enough to be gained. Risks too great. I don't know why Nolan got himself some pills and swallowed the works, but that's how it must have been."

Jericho looked up slowly from his partly demolished slab of sirloin. "Counsel for the defense is eloquent," he said. "You want to make it quite clear to me that I'll be wasting my time churning up the suggestion that Nolan was murdered. If I could make it stick, three quarters of a million bucks might go down the drain, plus a couple of careers, plus a few good solid jobs like your own. If you had any doubts about what happened to Nolan, would you turn your back on these doubts, Al?"

Al's tired eyes met Jericho's steadily. "That's a fair question," he said. "And the answer is, I don't honestly know. In our business we use the word 'integrity' very freely. But who has any? Maybe I'd turn my back on doubts. I don't think—and I say think—I'd turn my back on facts. Do you have any facts, Jericho?"

"What are facts to me may not be facts to you," Jericho

said. He cut himself a slice of steak with a razor-sharp knife. "Nolan's paintings represent a fact to me—the fact that he had a great talent, was full of energy and hope and drive and belief in himself. That he was coming on strong. That to me is a fact. He had a rather extraordinary girl on his team, and I rather imagine his sex life was something we might all envy. He had every reason to want to live and no reason on earth to want to die. To me those are facts, and until somebody proves to me that he bought himself sleeping pills and inhaled the whole bottle, they'll stay facts. I say that these facts indicate that someone slipped him something in a drink at Zelda's place and that he just did manage to get home before it caught up with him and killed him."

Al brought his fist down on the table. "So you're going to throw us to the wolves before you've been able to prove anything!"

"I'm not interested in press releases, friend," Jericho said, a touch of hardness in his voice. "The only thing I care about is the truth about Tommy Nolan. When I lay hands on it, I'm going to clear his name." He grinned. "Maybe you'll get your show on before I come up with the answers. I suspect that if forty million people have looked at Zelda on TV before I can drop my bomb, you couldn't care less what happens to her and her mob afterward. Your personal future depends on your getting this show on tape and before the public without troubles. Right?"

"Right," Al said, his voice low.

"Maybe we'll both get lucky," Jericho said. . . .

It was daylight when we finally walked out of Zirato's. Al and his Lillian took a taxi to parts unspecified. Jericho drove me to my apartment just off Irving Place. He didn't seem to be in the mood for talking. When we arrived at my door, he asked me if I'd mind taking charge of Nolan's painting.

"My studio in the Mews may not be the safest place in the world for it to be," he said.

"You think—"

"I think the pleasure I got in making an ass out of Master Ferrick may turn out to be a little expensive. My own pictures I can paint again. Nolan can't."

"You can get protection for your paintings!"

He didn't seem to hear me. "Keep in touch, Hally," he said. "If I'm unreachable for too long, check in with Pascal."

One of Jericho's good friends in the city is a policeman. His name is Pascal, and he's probably one of the best homicide men the force has ever had. He is a big, burly, pipe-smoking man who looks slow and slightly puzzled a good part of the time. He also looks like what he is—a man with the tenacity of a bulldog. He used to say that inspiration and hunch have no place in a police investigation. "You just check and check and check until something doesn't check," he'd say, "and then you're in."

It was to Pascal's apartment on the West Side that Jericho went after dropping me. He rang the buzzer in the lobby persistently until finally there was a response and Pascal's voice came over the house phone. When Jericho spoke his name, the buzzer clicked and he went in and up the one flight to the second floor. Pascal, his thick dark hair silvered at the temples, was wrapped in a flannel dressing gown. He was obviously a man who had been dredged up out of a solid sleep, but he offered no complaint.

"Nice to see you, Johnny," he said. No comment on the hour. When a friend needed Pascal, he was there. "Drink? Coffee? Take five minutes for it to percolate."

"Coffee would be fine."

Jericho stood looking around the book-lined living room. Pascal was a hound for history and biography, and he bought everything new that was well recommended but seldom got the time to read what he had bought. Someday, when he had retired—God forbid!

Pascal came back from the kitchen where he'd plugged in his coffeepot. "So you've put your foot into what?" he asked. He sat down in his own armchair, motioned Jericho to a matching one, and began to fill his pipe from a cedar-lined humidor.

"An artist named Tommy Nolan," Jericho said.

"Suicide," Pascal said, not looking up from his pipe filling.

"Maybe not."

"It just happens," Pascal said, a faint smile tugging at the corner of his mouth, "the matter came across my desk yesterday afternoon. It's pretty well checked out, Johnny. Popular-brand sleeping pills—the pink ones. Maybe eighteen—twenty. He'd been at a party—pop singer named

Zelda Rankin. But then you know all that, don't you?"

"Yes. I'm not impressed with the kind of job your boys did on it," Jericho said.

"My boys only in the sense that we are all cops," Pascal said. "The investigation wasn't mine. It was passed on to me to look over because there are big names in the background—Trans American Broadcasting, Helstrom Cosmetics, big money lying around everywhere. The Commissioner imagines I'm impressive when the big shots start flapping their wings. I was alerted. The investigation looked solid enough to me. Where did they miss?"

"They didn't look at Nolan's paintings," Jericho said.

"Oh?"

"They didn't look at Nolan's girl—not intelligently. I believe one of them pinched her fanny and invited her to dinner."

"Nasty old man," Pascal said, grinning.

"If you'd been on the job, you'd have asked yourself what the motive for suicide could possibly have been."

"Girl is that much of a dish?" Pascal asked, still grinning. Then he sobered. "Motives for suicide are harder to come by than for other crimes," he said. "He wasn't broke, I know from the report. Just made a handsome TV deal. No chronic diseases, according to the M.E. But what lies in the cellar and the subcellar and the sub-subcellar of the mind? Who knows? Not you. Maybe his psychiatrist, if he had one."

"Did he?"

"Not that we know of." Pascal lit his pipe. "Suicides are

so often the result of a sudden, irrational impulse."

"This fellow wanted to live and had everything to live for."

"You say. But let's get realistic. The report says a taxi picked him up about a block from Zelda Rankin's apartment—outside a drugstore. The druggist says he came in, obviously tight, and said he was going to need something for a hang-over. The druggist says he sold him a bottle of bromo. He probably did. What else he sold him he isn't saying."

"You're suggesting sleeping pills?"

"It's possible. It's likely, since he made no other stop. The taxi took him to his place. He was so tight by then he needed help getting the front door unlocked—but sober enough to pay the taximan and give him a dollar's tip. He is remembered for that."

"The paper said he stopped somewhere for a drink."

"Guesswork, before they found the driver," Pascal said. "Now it seems likely he took the pills in the cab and tossed the bottle or box out the window."

"I don't think so," Jericho said.

Pascal took a comfortable pull at his pipe. "So tell me what you've invented, Johnny."

So Jericho told his story from start to finish. Pascal is a good listener. He interrupted only once, when Jericho came to the encounter with Ferrick.

"Don't you ever pick a fight with someone your own size?" he asked.

"Ferrick's no pushover," Jericho said sharply.

64

"My dear Johnny, that's exactly what I meant. Ferrick and his mob of young fancies are much too tough for one large, belligerent artist. I think you need to take a crash course in Ferrick and Company. You've probably had the only experience you'll ever have of standing toe to toe with one of them. From now on they'll come at you out of the dark, always from behind; you'll need to brace yourself on subway platforms, to stay out of self-service elevators in small buildings. I could go on and on."

"You trying to scare me?" Jericho asked.

"Hopefully," Pascal said. He sighed. "You and I are romantics, Johnny. We still believe in nice, straightforward crime—murder for money, or revenge, or from jealousy. You only have to spend ten minutes a day reading the papers to know there's a whole new variety of monster on the loose. Was the lump of sugar that fellow at the next table just put in his coffee soaked in LSD? Is he apt to jump up from the table and shoot you, scattering your brains into your bacon and eggs for no reason whatsoever? Motive plays a much less important part in crime these days than it used to. People just seem to explode, without reason."

"My point," Jericho said.

Pascal's eyebrows rose. "I was trying to say it may not be possible to find a reasonable motive for Nolan's suicide. You're trying to have me say that someone of Zelda's crew could have poisoned his liquor without having any real reason for doing it."

"Well?"

65

Pascal was silent for a moment. "It's possible," he said slowly. "Though how somebody could slip eighteen or twenty pills into his drink without his knowing it—"

"The powder out of eighteen capsules," Jericho said.

"Vile tasting," Pascal said.

"He was very angry," Jericho said. "He could have tossed off a drink without paying much attention to the fact it tasted bad. He certainly didn't expect to be murdered—just violated as an artist."

"How can we, the police, prove any of this unless someone in Zelda's group decided to talk?" Pascal asked. "Our facts don't justify an investigation. He went into a drugstore, obviously stoned, and bought a bottle of antacid. A taxi driver took him home and helped him unlock his front door. He went up to his apartment, undressed, hung his clothes neatly on a chair, and went to bed. He woke up feeling terrible. He staggered into the next room to telephone for help, fell, and struck his head on the table. It was enough of a blow to prevent him from struggling up and trying for the phone again. He died where he lay. You say that's all mullarkey because his sex life was good and his paintings were full of life. I am therefore, as a policeman, asked to ignore all that and assume he was murdered because he wouldn't become an artistic whore for television gold. Go home to bed, Johnny."

"You want to believe the obvious because you can close the case," Jericho said.

"Let's have no low blows from you at five in the morning," Pascal said. "And when you do get to bed, make sure

66

you've double-locked your studio door. You might wake up with a crowd of long-haired young men burning holes in the soles of your feet with cigarette lighters."

Jericho got up from his chair and walked over to the window. A sanitation truck was picking up garbage cans across the way.

"I've spent a very full life following my instincts about the bastards of this world," he said. "We're all expected to walk away from this. I can't do it, Pascal. Somebody knows the truth about this, and I'm going to get that somebody to talk. I don't know what it will take, but I'll keep at it until someone gives. I didn't know Nolan, but he's entitled to a defense."

"I don't know how you've managed to live so long," Pascal said dryly. "But you're a pleasure, even at five o'clock in the morning. What do you want me to do for you?"

Jericho turned. "You can do something that I can't do," he said. "Your boys aren't putting the heat on that drug-store man because experience tells them it's hopeless. If he sold sleeping pills without a prescription, it will be almost impossible to nail him. My guess is he didn't. My guess also is that Zelda Rankin, Perry Lewis, and Company are up to their scrawny necks in narcotics. For once can't you go after the rich ones instead of some poor, delinquent Harlem kid who robs the local candy store to get money for his pusher?"

Pascal shook his head wearily. "I can't promise," he said. "I'll make noises in the right places, but I can't prom-

67

ise anything."

"Your loud noises are the best I can hope for," Jericho said. "Thanks for listening."

Pascal heaved himself up out of his chair. "A long time ago I learned it was useless to suggest that you not take absurd risks, Johnny," he said. "This time it's too late. You've already made yourself a target for Ferrick and his rosy-cheeked boys. You wouldn't like to go to—say, Spain—on a painting trip, would you?"

"I can't avoid him if I'm going to twist a few arms in Zelda's world, can I?"

"Go home," Pascal said, "but keep looking in your rear-view mirror. I'll let you know if Narcotics has anything at all on Zelda's crowd."

Fifteen minutes later Jericho had garaged his car and walked into Jefferson Mews toward his studio. It was still pretty early for any activity in the area. Two or three houses down Jericho saw Mike Guffanti, the ex-prize fighter who acted as janitor for several of the buildings in the Mews, hosing down the sidewalk. He waved and Mike waved back.

The street door to the building where Jericho lived was almost never locked. An elderly woman writer who occupied the floor above the studio never could find her door key. Whenever she went out, she put the front door on the latch. If someone locked it while she was out, she would arrive home and start ringing every doorbell in the place till someone let her in. Jericho and the other tenants had finally given up, so the street door was perpetually on the latch.

Jericho paused at the door and looked back around the Mews. Pascal was not an alarmist. Jericho had literally checked his rearview mirror on the trip downtown, and now he was, in effect, doing it again. Jefferson Mews, except for Mike Guffanti appeared to be asleep.

Jericho went in and climbed the stairs to the second floor. The hallway was dark except for a dim light bulb at the far end. The fixture at this end of the hall hadn't worked for weeks, in spite of repeated promises from Mike Guffanti. But even in the semidarkness Jericho recognized the girl and felt a sharp jolt in the pit of his stomach. Patricia O'Hanlon Barry was leaning against his door as if she was asleep.

"You took long enough," she said.

She was wearing a trench coat belted in around her slim waist. Her violet eyes seemed to burn in the murk. The gold hair hung loose and lovely about her shoulders. Jericho told me afterward that he felt both a cascading excitement and anger. He stood close to her, looking down.

"I know that sex is here to stay," he said, "but aren't you rather pushing things, ma'am?"

She hit him a good stinging slap on his bearded cheek. "Is that what you've had me standing here an hour for?" she said, her voice unsteady with rage. "I thought you were on the level. I got your message and came. Now if

**69**

you'll just get out of my way."

"Just a minute," he said, checking her with his big hands on her shoulder. "What message?"

"Your friend from Zirato's told me you wanted me to come here, so I—"

"What friend?"

"How should I know? He just said you'd asked him to call. Naturally I—"

She was interrupted by the sound of shattering glass from inside the studio. Jericho's head turned sharply away from her. Then, suddenly, he whisked her up into his arms and went charging down the hall. Before he reached the stair, the building was shaken by an enormous explosion. Jericho dove for the corner and landed so that his huge body was covering the girl. He looked back and saw that his studio door had been blown off its hinges.

He looked down at the lovely face so close to him. "I think, ma'am, you saved my life," he said.

Her smile was so close he could almost taste it.

"I think, sir, it was your own puritanical morality," she said. "If you'd invited me in instead of arguing with me about why I was there—"

# Part 2

# One

Jefferson Mews was now very definitely awake. Up-stairs someone began to scream, regularly, like a ticking clock. Outside people shouted from open windows. A piercing female voice took up the chant of "Fire! Fire!"

Jericho was on his feet, helping Pat Barry up from where she'd been literally thrown in the corner by him. Behind them someone came charging up the stairs from the street level. It was Mike Guffanti, the custodian, car-rying a large brass fire extinguisher.

"Thank God you're okay, Johnny!" he said. "What the hell happened?"

He didn't wait for an answer. He scrambled over a pile of smoking debris into Jericho's studio. Jericho was at his heels.

"Easy with that extinguisher, Mike. If that stuff gets on pictures—"

The damage inside the studio could have been worse from Jericho's point of view. Someone had obviously tossed a crude version of a Molotov cocktail through the skylight. The homemade bomb had skidded across the floor and exploded directly against the heavy door. It could have landed in the stacks of paintings or the huge collection of drawings in wooden cabinets against the far wall. It could have started an uncontrollable fire. And, if Jericho hadn't paused in the hall to talk to Pat Barry, it could have ended his career with a grim finality.

The thick smoke that spiraled up through the smashed skylight seemed to come from the remnants of the bomb itself. Mike Guffanti, square-shouldered and efficient in crisis, swept up the smoking pieces and dumped them in Jericho's garbage pail and carried them out into the yard, leaving Jericho to aim the fire extinguisher at a few smoldering spots in the floor and the smashed doorway. The shouting and yelling were growing in volume, punctuated now by the sound of an approaching police siren.

Patricia O'Hanlon Barry appeared in the doorway. She looked completely unruffled. But the heat of anger burned in the violet eyes, turning them dark.

"They meant to kill you," she said.

"To shake me up at any rate," Jericho said.

"I waited inside here for you because there was a small riot in the Mews about forty-five minutes ago," the girl said.

"Riot?"

"An army of children," Pat said. "Mopheaded boys, girls

74

in bell-bottom pants, some black-jacketed motorcycle boys—all fifteen or sixteen years old. They were led by some Beatle types with guitars. All singing and yelling. I was spotted for some kind of tramp waiting for a customer, and they shouted dirty words at me. I came inside to get out of trouble. People were yelling at them from windows to get out of here. They began heaving things at the people in the windows. It wasn't pretty. One of them could have come back and thrown that bomb at the largest piece of glass he saw."

"Could be," Jericho said. He aimed the extinguisher at a smoking section of the smashed door. He didn't sound convinced.

"You don't think so?" Pat asked.

"No, I don't think so," Jericho said. He turned his bright blue eyes her way. "I didn't have time out there in the hall to make it very clear to you that I sent you no message."

"You weren't at Zirato's?"

"I was there. But I didn't ask anyone to call you. I regret to say I wasn't even thinking about you. Not much, that is."

"We were both meant to get it?"

"What did the caller sound like?" Jericho asked, ignoring the question.

"Man. Soft, cultivated voice. Late as it was, would I please come to your studio in Jefferson Mews at once? You had just left Zirato's."

"You were still at Nolan's place?"

She nodded. "I hadn't told you where else you could

reach me. I wanted to know what happened at Zelda's. What did happen?"

"Not tellable now, because we are about to have the police." The siren had come to a moaning halt outside the building. Cars weren't allowed in the Mews, except police cars. "I think for the moment we adopt your theory. This was an outcome of the riot you described."

Captain Welch of the local precinct station was ready enough to accept the riot theory. Like every other reasonably solid citizen in the Greenwich Village area, he was bugged by the Friday-night invasion of children. They came pouring out of the subway stations early in the evening and literally took over the Village, staring at the pop art, necking on the street corners and in hallways, chanting and singing.

"They've turned the Village into a vast amusement park on the weekends," Welch said. "They sound like some aboriginal tribe on the warpath. They push the local residents off the sidewalk, screaming insults at them; they've driven out the tourists who used to bring a profitable trade into the cafés and restaurants. We have fifty additional cops on the street on Friday night, but we can't control 'em. Some of them are really just children—ten, twelve years old."

"They often toss around high explosives?" Jericho asked quietly.

"No," the police captain said, "but we've been waiting for something like this. The hysteria grows higher and higher with each passing week. Sooner or later we've felt it would have to give somewhere at the seams. I'd like you and Miss Barry to come down to the station and make a full statement for us."

"I'd rather not," Jericho said politely. "There are a good many thousand dollars' worth of paintings in here. I don't propose to leave them, unprotected, without any ceiling or lockable front door."

Welch nodded. He looked tired. "Later will do. We'll have to make a house-to-house check, hoping someone saw one of these kids come back—or stick around after the mob left. Not much hope, I'm afraid. Somehow they all look alike. People don't really see 'em any more as individuals—like you can't distinguish one cockroach from another in your sink."

Welch disappeared to begin his dreary and almost certainly unproductive round of the other apartments in the Mews. Jericho reached in his pocket for his pipe, looking slowly around the wreckage with a quick, assessing eye. Miraculously, except for some smoke damage which could be repaired, his pictures were intact. Pat had perched herself on the arm of a chair and was looking curiously around the studio.

"You didn't answer me before," she said. "I was meant to get it along with you?"

"It's pretty obvious, isn't it?" A slow, smoldering anger was beginning to eat at Jericho.

"It's all connected with Tommy?" Pat asked.

Almost reluctantly he told her of his visit to the Hell

Hole and his encounter with Ferrick. "I've been warned by experts that I can expect bad trouble from him," he concluded. "I think this is the beginning. You were responsible for getting me into the act, so you, it seems, are to be included in his pay-off."

"I see," she said quietly.

He grinned at her. "Scared?"

"Yes."

"Good girl," he said. "I haven't much use for people who haven't sense enough to be afraid of danger. I seemed to have opened a rather poisonous can of peas by flexing my muscles a little too much."

"So now?" she asked.

He glanced up at the smashed skylight. "It'll be days before my landlord gets around to fixing that. I have an affection for my paintings and drawings, so I can't leave them here. I'll get my gallery people to take charge of them until the all-clear sounds. Meanwhile I'll have to find myself a temporary bed."

"You can have Tommy's place," she said. "But that doesn't quite answer what I meant by my question. So now, what do *I* do? I've defended my virtue from quite a few predatory males in my time, Johnny, but not killers! Somebody bombs your roof out and you worry what's going to happen to your pictures. I worry about what's going to happen to me!"

He looked at her thoughtfully. There are times when Jericho fails to understand that not all people react to danger the way he does. To him danger is simply a stimu-

78

lating challenge.

"You run or you fight," he said, as if that solved everything.

She flared up at him. "You big baboon! I asked you to protect Tommy's work from that television crowd, not to start a Hatfield-McCoy! I know all about you! I suppose you're feeling just great at the moment with new dragons to slay. But stop talking to me like a character out of Batman! I'm in the middle of your personal Waring mixer, mister, and I damn well need instructions on how to protect myself!"

It occurred to him that she was very close to tears.

"Pat, I'm sorry," he said gently. He waved vaguely at the wrecked room. "I guess this has left me a little overstimulated. Where do you live?"

"I have a two-room apartment around the corner from Tommy's place. I met him, of all places, in the little store where he bought Colombian coffee."

"How do you eat?" he asked.

"If you laugh, I'll tear that red beard out by the roots," she said, laughing in spite of herself.

"Scout's honor," he said.

"I write a syndicated column of advice to the unhappily married," she said. "I have never been married. I inherited the job from a sixty-year-old bachelor who has retired to his vegetable garden in northwest Connecticut. I am a very wise woman—in print. But I don't know how to handle a bomb-throwing queer, and it looks as though I needed to know!"

"You told Hallam that you were living with Nolan," he said.

"I did not! I told him, very specifically, that I was not living with him. I said I made love with him, which is quite different, and which you, as a long-term bachelor, should understand without my drawing diagrams. And what has that got to do with how I protect myself?"

"Is there some place you can go for a while, out of the city?" he asked. "Family somewhere?" It was the kind of advice people were always giving him and which he never took.

"I will not be driven out of my home," she said, her voice shaking, "or out of my city, or out of my job. I think I should walk out on you and go to the police and tell them the truth about all this. I'm entitled to protection, aren't I? You never once mentioned to Captain Welch that there could be any real reason for all this! You want to play lone wolf. Go ahead, but I—"

"Now quiet down," he said. "Just before I got home I'd spent three-quarters of an hour with the smartest policeman in New York. He knows about Ferrick. And he'll know about this very shortly. I didn't tell Welch because I want my man Pascal to handle any police end of this. Would you feel a little easier if we went to see him?"

For the first time the fighting edge went out of her voice. The tears were very close. "One doesn't feel very safe depending on you, Johnny," she said. "You expect miracles."

"Don't we all?" he said, sounding vapidly cheerful.

80

"I don't," she said, her eyes averted, "because I know they don't exist. How can you make it safe for me, Johnny? Is there any way you can get this Ferrick lunatic off my back?"

Jericho told me afterward he was a little surprised by this small crack-up. He'd expected a kind of casual courage.

" 'Lunatic' is the right word for him," he said. "We just have to watch our step."

She turned to him, and he was shocked by the change in her face. It was bloodless, lines about the corners of her eyes he hadn't known were there. "I don't have time for games, Johnny," she said. "I only have time for one anxiety."

"What are you talking about?"

She turned and ran into the bedroom behind the studio. He heard a great strangling sob and then the terrible sound of uncontrolled weeping.

Jericho thought he understood. She'd been calm enough at the moment of the explosion, even ready with a small quip—about his puritanical morals. She'd shown no signs of distress while Captain Welch was with them. It was only when it began to dawn on her that she, too, had been a part of the bomber's target that she'd begun to crack. Jericho had seen this kind of thing a thousand times—the human being who is cool and efficient under fire who goes to pieces when the immediate danger is past.

The kindest thing was to let her get control without his getting into the act, he thought. He stood in the center of

81

the room, filling his black curve-stemmed pipe. Ferrick wasn't just a brawling sadist. This had been a carefully calculated attempt at a double murder. He wondered about the mob of teen-agers. They'd never found their way into Jefferson Mews before. Was their coming tonight a coincidence or had Ferrick used them? A twenty-dollar bill would buy an awful lot of red vino, the favorite drink of the mopheads. "Toss this can of soup through the skylight, kids, when the red beard comes home—and drink hearty." One thing stuck in Jericho's craw. It was hard to imagine that Ferrick, elegant in his in wardrobe, his money worries taken care of by Zelda, dining and drinking in the most expensive places in town, would have a homemade bomb hidden away somewhere in case he got mad at someone. You didn't put a highly efficient bomb like that together in five minutes. Everything had been so carefully planned. Pat had been brought in—and yet Jericho hadn't had any connection with Pat until about forty minutes before he'd put the slug on Ferrick. Ferrick couldn't have wasted a single minute after he came to on the chair in the Hell Hole, draped with flowers. The footwork had been notable!

In the bedroom there seemed to be no letup in the spasmodic sobs. Enough was enough, Jericho thought. He went into the bedroom. She was curled up like a small child, her face buried in his pillow. He sat down beside her and put a huge, comforting hand on her shoulder.

"Look, baby, it's all over for the moment," he said. "You'd better try to get pulled together."

He could feel her muscles tense, and then, unexpectedly, she rolled over on her back and lay there, staring up at the ceiling. Her eyes were red and swollen.

"This is the first time in my life I've ever lost control like this in front of anyone else," she said.

"There's a first for everything," he said cheerfully. He saw that her hands were gripping the bedcover so fiercely the knuckles were white.

"I guess when you take off the mask it's time for the moment of truth. I must be a sight!"

"You look like a scared kid," he said.

"I am scared, Johnny. So scared! So desperately scared!"

"It was a bad moment," he said.

"Not long ago I had the moment that tops that—and all others!" she said. "Johnny, do you have the guts to take on a very special, private burden?"

"Protecting you from Ferrick? Sure," he said.

She pushed herself up to a sitting position, and he thought he had never seen a face so anguished. "I suddenly know I can't go on without help," she said. "Tommy gave me that help without knowing it, but now—"

"Let's knock off the riddles," he said.

She looked straight at him. "Johnny, I'm going to die," she said. "A year—fifteen months."

He just stared at her.

An ice-cold hand reached out for his. "It's a blood thing," she said. "Like leukemia. They don't know anything to do about it. For perhaps a year there won't be any severe problem—perhaps a little less energy. *I want*

83

*that year, Johnny!* I want to live it! I want to savor every moment of it! I don't want to fight some idiot, just to have the chance!"

His stomach muscles felt knotted. He told me later he found it hard to breathe. She had seemed so very much alive, so much the mistress of her own way of life.

She read his mind. "You thought I was some sort of very modern, free and easy original," she said. "It's a part I've played, played with Tommy who never knew. Before it was too late, Johnny, I needed love, I needed affection, I needed to taste all the joys of life I thought I had a right to expect. Marriage I can't have. Children I can't have. Tommy Nolan wanted no bonds. And so we made love, and it was good, and I tried to pretend to him it was all I wanted—because it was all he wanted. It was right for him, and he thought it was right for me. I made him think it. Someday I would wake up and know that the time had come and I'd walk out on him, and he'd think the race had been run. He always said that someday, without having to give a reason, one of us would walk out on the other. Poor darling, he walked out when he didn't intend to. Johnny, I want this year! I want it!"

"You'll have it," he said, his voice harsh, knowing that he hadn't the faintest idea how he could guarantee such a thing.

"No one else must know. I can't stand pity, Johnny. I've told you because somehow I know you wouldn't subject me to pity."

He leaned forward and kissed her gently on the forehead. "We'll make it a hell of a year," he said. "We'll make it a fun time."

She let herself down on the pillow again, her eyes closed. She looked exhausted. "Thank you, Johnny," she whispered.

How do you not feel pity? he asked himself. . . .

My telephone woke me about a quarter to ten. I knew nothing about the bombing in the Mews. I knew nothing of Pat Barry's tragedy. I had slept without dreams. I wasn't very deeply concerned by Jericho's brush with Ferrick. Jericho knows how to take care of himself in head-on encounters.

My caller was Al Stover, the TAB man. "Did I wake you?" he asked.

"High time," I said. A soft rain was falling outside my bedroom window. It was an ideal day to stay home and wrestle with the problems of my novel.

"I'm sorry about Jericho," Al said. "You wouldn't have any idea where to reach him, would you?"

"I can call him at his studio and get him to call you," I said. "It would be worth my life to give you his unlisted number."

Al sounded puzzled. "He isn't there, of course. Hally, you haven't heard about the bombing? It's been on the radio all morning."

"Bombing?" I sat bolt upright in bed.

Al gave me a run-down. Rioting kids was the story the papers and the radio and TV stations were giving out. Al didn't buy it and neither did I. "He was lucky," Al said. "He had stopped out in the hallway to talk to Patricia Barry, who was evidently waiting for him. That delay kept him from getting the bomb right in his face when he opened the door. Somebody was watching for him and timed it exactly, except Jericho was delayed in the hall. I thought he might have gotten in touch with you."

"He hasn't," I said. "He's probably doing something about his paintings. Duckworth Galleries handles his stuff. We could try Henry Duckworth. What about the Barry girl? You tried her?"

"Both her own apartment and Nolan's," Al said. "No dice. The point is, Hally, there's hell to pay here."

"Here?"

"My shop. Trans American," he said. "The big brass and the attorney for Helstrom Cosmetics. Some decisions have to be made, and if I can't find Jericho or Miss Barry, you might be able to help me. Can you come up to the Trans American Building in a hurry? Conference room on the twenty-fifth floor."

"What can I do for you?"

"You know the score and you know Jericho," Al said. His voice was ragged. "It's very important to me, Hally."

"I'll come," I said. "Three-quarters of an hour."

I hung up and dialed the studio in the Mews. No answer. I called the Duckworth Gallery and got Henry Duckworth, who was Jericho's friend and agent. Henry told me Jericho was involved in transferring a truckload of paintings from the studio to the Duckworth warehouse.

86

He'd get word to him to call me. I gave him the TAB number in case Jericho wasn't in touch in the next ten minutes.

I dressed in a hurry, swilling down a cup of lukewarm reheated coffee in the process. I was lucky, considering the rain, with a taxi, and I walked into the conference room at the TAB building exactly forty minutes after I'd hung up on Al Stover.

The conference room is the essence of big-business cliché. There is the long, polished conference table, with the neatly placed pads and pencils at each place, a thick oriental rug that made you feel as if you were walking on moss, the silver ash trays, the neatly framed reproductions of Currier and Ives prints around the wall, a telephone instrument at each place in case a conference call was the order of business, silver cigarette boxes, humidors of expensive cigars, pitchers of ice water accompanied by tall monogrammed glasses, a large portable bar in a far corner of the room. The electric clock with its relentlessly moving red second hand showed me it was exactly four minutes to eleven as I walked into the room.

I knew most of the people who were already seated at the table. Al gave me a grateful little wave of the hand as I came in. He was seated to the left of the meeting's chairman, who was Nick Glass, program chairman for TAB. Glass is a dark, never-smiling little Napoleon, cordially hated by everyone who works for him, and at the same time reluctantly admired for his professional judgments. Rich Ragsdale sat at Glass's right, his cropped head lowered, his eyes apparently closed above their heavy pouches. Everyone but Ragsdale wore neat dark business suits, the Madison Avenue uniform. Ragsdale had on a faded pair of blue jeans, a maroon sports shirt, and a wrinkled seersucker jacket. He was always carefully nonconformist.

Perry Lewis was slumped deep in a chair next to Al, looking as though he'd been reluctantly pulled out of bed, the ravages of last night's drinking obvious. Maury Zimmerman, TAB's wizard salesman, grinned at me happily. He had been responsible for my original involvement with Zelda Rankin. The two public relations men were there, fiddling nervously with their pencils and pads, Marty Farmer for Zelda's crowd, and Mike Crowley for Helstrom Cosmetics. PR men are always hair-trigger ready to take notes. The man I didn't know by sight, a gray, hawk-faced, humorless gent, turned out to be Max Morrison, Helstrom's lawyer.

"Thank you for coming, Mr. Hallam," Nick Glass said, and waved me to a chair next to Maury Zimmerman. Maury gave me a little pat on the knee.

"You should have had this session for your piece on Zelda," he whispered. "Fasten your safety belt."

"We have all read the profile you wrote on Zelda, Mr. Hallam," Glass said, "and we all like it very much."

The chorus of yes men muttered hasty approval. All but the lawyer, Morrison, who looked at me as if I were some unpleasant specimen under a microscope.

"Today is Saturday," Glass said.

They all muttered quickly that it was indeed Saturday.

"On Monday we are scheduled to go before the cameras with one of the most expensive and outstanding specials that TAB has ever made. In the last forty-eight hours several disturbing things have happened which make us wonder whether radical changes in the whole plan may not be necessary. We need your help and advice."

"I couldn't begin to advise you," I said. "Television is a foreign country to me."

"You at least admit it," Ragsdale said, without opening his eyes.

"The unfortunate suicide of Nolan," Glass said, ignoring the director, "brought us face to face with our first set of doubts. Should we proceed with the use of his paintings in the special, or would his suicide cast a pall on the proceedings? We decided, I think properly, that we would go ahead as planned. Nolan's paintings, speaking as they do for modern youth, deserved the opportunity to convey their message to our vast audience."

The yes men muttered eager agreement.

"There are, however, sudden complications," Glass said, his scowl dark.

The yes men nodded, all scowling.

"Rich Ragsdale has devised a startlingly effective use of Nolan's paintings as a background for Zelda Rankin's performance," Glass said. He raised his right hand, and Al instantly poured a glass of water and put it into that hand. Glass sipped and put down the glass without a glance at Al. "In the beginning," he went on, "our Mr. Stover agreed to certain contractual arrangements which we approved, despite my grave misgivings. Nolan was to have a veto power over the way his pictures were used."

The yes men looked at Al as though he should have known better. Naughty, naughty!

Ragsdale's eyes opened slit-wide. "It was a perfectly good arrangement," he said. "Nolan was a man with real artistic integrity. He was also a realist. He knew we were selling Zelda first and his paintings second."

"Or third," Maury Zimmerman said cheerfully. "Ahead of the paintings, and perhaps on an equal footing with Zelda, we were selling Rich Ragsdale." He glanced at Morrison, the lawyer, for confirmation. Morrison gave him back the Mount Rushmore stare.

"Let's lay off the hog wallow," Perry said, twisting uncomfortably in his chair. "You were selling Zelda. Period!"

Ragsdale turned his narrowed slits on Glass. "You want my comment or not, Nick?"

"Please, Rich," Glass said.

"When the day comes that the director is more important than the star, God help us all," Perry Lewis said.

Ragsdale pushed back his chair. "I've got too much to do to sit around listening to that kind of crap," he said.

"Please, Rich!" Glass said. He glared at Perry, who seemed to retire into himself, smiling a sour, secret smile. He had made a small score. He had irritated the great Ragsdale.

90

"To repeat," Ragsdale said wearily, "Nolan was an all-right guy. We had our disagreements. I kidded him a little too long, I guess, about changing one of his paintings to look like Zelda. I wouldn't have dreamed of doing it. I have integrity, too, you know. It would be unthinkable to tamper with Nolan's work."

"Your point, Rich?" Glass said.

"My point is that the contract was a perfectly good one, so long as it involved Nolan and me. Now we are confronted with something quite different. Nolan left an artistic executor—some balmy babe who writes a column for the lovelorn.

That was news to me at that point.

"She turned out not to be a total idiot," Ragsdale went on. "She's not an artist or a director and she knows it. She calls in a highly reputable artist to stand in for her. Your friend Jericho, Mr. Hallam." He glanced at me as though I was suddenly the villain of the piece. "I would buy Jericho's judgment about paintings, and his taste, and perhaps even his ideas. But within fifteen minutes of his taking on the job, Jericho gets himself into an intolerable personal feud with one of Zelda's friends. Within a few hours his studio is bombed and we're all over the front pages and the TV and radio. If Jericho stays in the picture, we've had it. The publicity will be intolerable. The whole concept and quality of the special will be destroyed by screaming headlines, back-stage dirt, and God knows what new idiocies devised by Jericho and Don Ferrick. Right now they're saying it was a gang of mop-haired juvenile delinquents who bombed Jericho's studio. But you and I know, and pretty soon every columnist and reporter in the country will know, that it was Ferrick who tried to get Jericho. Our only chance at this moment is to get Jericho to pull out and persuade Miss Barry to appoint someone else to represent Nolan. The headlines will then stay with Jericho and Ferrick and won't be tied into our project." He turned to me. "That's why you're here, Hallam. Can you persuade Jericho to withdraw? Can you persuade Miss Barry to see the light?"

"You know we're not trying to go behind Jericho's back," Al Stover said. "You know we've tried all morning to reach him."

"We have to make our decision," Glass said. "Since Jericho isn't available, we need a solid opinion from you. Can he be persuaded?"

"Don't strain yourself, Hallam," Perry Lewis said. "What you think doesn't matter. Jericho stays."

Heads turned Perry's way, as though a camera had stopped in the middle of filming the spectators at a ping-pong game.

"Say that again," Glass said, his voice cold and hard.

Perry seemed to untangle himself as he reached for a cigarette. He smiled blandly at the Big Shot. "Jericho stays," he said. "I like him. I like what he did to Don-boy last night. He stays."

For the first time since my arrival, the lawyer for Helstrom spoke. His voice was harsh, as if anger had been churning behind that rock-hard exterior. "Contract-wise, it doesn't matter what you say, Mr. Lewis."

Perry turned his dissipated faun's face. "My baby could get sick," he said.

It was, I gathered, the well-known refrain of a very unpopular song.

"We'll sue!" Morrison said.

"Can you collect damages for a chronic bronchitis?" Perry asked. "Jericho stays."

"Now look, Perry—" Al Stover tried.

"He stays, boy," Perry said.

Glass moved slightly, as though he was breakable. "The attack on Jericho was attempted murder," he said. "We have to get clear of that, Perry. We can't be remotely involved with it."

"What connection do you have with Greenwich Village delinquents?" Perry asked blandly.

"Oh, for Christ sake, stop kidding around, Perry," Ragsdale said. "You and I know it was Ferrick."

"I say it wasn't," Perry said. "I say it couldn't have been."

"How do you know that?" Glass asked, leaning forward, almost eagerly.

"Because," Perry said jauntily, "he was in bed with my wife."

There was a mass sigh that sounded like wind in the tops of pine trees.

"What an incredible thing to say!" Morrison exploded.

"You can't know that, Perry," Ragsdale said. "You were passed out cold." He looked around the table. "It's stand-ard practice. Perry passes out every night. He only knows what happens after that by rumor."

Perry giggled. "Only I know the times I pass out and the times I pretend to pass out," he said.

"And which was it last night?" Ragsdale asked.

"That, boy, is for you to guess and for me to know," Perry said. "But if Don boy needs an alibi, Zelda will provide it. So you don't need to worry about a murder charge. It was Greenwich Village moppets."

After what seemed a very long silence Rich Ragsdale stood up. "I can't spend any more time here, Nick," he said to Glass. "I have a technical crew, cameramen, designer, and God knows who else waiting for me out in Brooklyn. Unless you decide to dump the show here and now, I have to leave you."

Glass looked at the lawyer for Helstrom Cosmetics.

"We have already spent a quarter of a million dollars in prepaid advertising," Morrison said. His face was grim. "Our pre-taping expenses, paid to you, run to nearly a hundred thousand. If you can't deliver what you've sold us, Mr. Glass, Helstrom Cosmetics will take legal steps to recover every cent they have so far expended, plus damages."

"What about a substitute show?" Glass asked.

Before Morrison could answer, Perry Lewis wagged an admonitory finger at the TAB executive. "We have a contract with you, Nick, for two hundred and fifty thousand dollars. Unless you can prove we have jeopardized your lily-white reputation in some fashion—in court, boy—

94

you'll be out that."

Glass looked suddenly old. "You'd better get to work, Rich," he said to Ragsdale. "I'll have to talk to the higher-ups. That'll be all for the rest of you—except you, Al, and you, Mr. Hallam, if you'd be good enough to stay behind for a few minutes."

Maury Zimmerman winked at me as he went out. The rest of them were funereal, except Perry Lewis. He cocked a bloodshot eye at me.

"You tell Jericho I love him," he said.

"He's had all his shots," I said, "for typhoid, beriberi. I guess he's safe."

"Funny man," Perry said, and sauntered out.

Al Stover hadn't moved from his chair at the table. He sat there with his hands covering his face. Glass was on his feet, storming up and down the far end of the room. He whirled on me as the door closed on the departed conferees.

"I thought we all performed very well, didn't you, Mr. Hallam?" he shouted at me. "Didn't you think I was good as the big-time executive? Didn't you think Morrison played the hard-boiled lawyer to perfection? Wasn't Rich the odd-ball director to a T? And isn't Perry perfect casting for the all-American jerk? We play our roles fine, don't you think? Even Al here is perfect for the unfairly punished Spaniel puppy!"

"If you'd taped it," I said, "you might have a better show than Zelda can put on for you."

"Oh God," Glass said. He went over to the portable bar

and poured himself a drink. He swung around to me again. "I have the feeling you're that rare person, someone we can talk to off the record. Am I right?"

"Jericho is involved in this. I have no secrets from him," I said.

Glass's eyes glittered. "I wish I'd seen him manhandle Don Ferrick. That long-haired creep has been running wild in this town for too long."

"It was pretty," I said.

"We're gambling huge sums of money, Hallam."

"You've put on turkeys before this," I said.

"Look, it's not a question of turkey," Glass said. "If Zelda and Ragsdale put on a bad show, it would bruise us some in terms of futures, but it wouldn't wreck us. What's involved here is the possibility of spending a quarter of a million bucks on a show we can never put on the air, a damage suit from Helstrom for all the money they've spent on promotion, plus the possibility of a neat little earth-shaking scandal. Before I eat lunch I've got to say yes or no. If you were in my shoes—"

"Which I most happily am not," I said. "One thing nobody mentioned at your four-star conference, Mr. Glass, is the very firm conviction that Jericho holds, that I hold, and that Miss Patricia Barry holds."

"What conviction?"

"That Tommy Nolan was murdered," I said.

He stared at me as though I'd suddenly gone idiot. "Say that again," he said.

"We think Nolan was murdered," I said. "Jericho thinks

96

somebody slipped him a Mickey at Zelda's that night and that he just did make it home to die."

"Did you know about this, Al?" Glass demanded.

Al nodded, his hands still covering his face. "I heard Jericho and Hally discussing it."

"And you didn't think it was worth mentioning to me?" Glass asked, ominously quiet.

"I thought it was a farfetched idea," Al said. "I thought you had enough troubles, Nick, without bothering you with Jericho's wild theory. The police have closed the case. It was a suicide."

"Oh, brother!" Glass said. "Does Jericho have anything on which to base his notion, Mr. Hallam?"

"Nothing that will stand up in court," I said. "Nolan's work doesn't suggest suicidal tendencies; his private life was happy and complete; he'd just made a nice deal with you which took care of any economic problems he might have."

"Ten G's," Glass muttered, as though it was tip money.

"That takes care of a lot of eating for an artist," I said.

"The police have written it off as suicide," Al said doggedly.

"Why don't you just drop Zelda's special and do something else for Helstrom Cosmetics?" I asked.

"Just pretend you didn't ask that," Glass said. "Thousands and thousands of dollars have already been spent on national advertising that's already not recallable—magazines that go to press weeks and months ahead of time. Contracts that aren't revokable, like seventy-five thousand dollars to Ragsdale that he has, in effect, already earned. An unbreakable balance to Zelda of a hundred and a half."

"Jericho isn't a show-off," I said. "He didn't turn Ferrick into a phony corpse just to show the world how large his biceps are. I think he means to keep putting the heat on Zelda and her crowd until somebody's foot slips."

"Or until he gets himself killed," Al said.

"Will he withdraw as Nolan's official representative on the show? At least that would sever any connection with us," Glass said.

"What about Perry Lewis? Would little Zelda really develop a chronic bronchitis if Jericho quits?" I asked.

Glass looked beaten. "As Major Bowes used to say," he said, " 'Round it goes, and where it comes out, nobody knows.' "

"Can you get Jericho here to talk to Nick or get Nick to Jericho?" Al asked.

"I can certainly try," I said, "but God knows where he is or what his next move is going to be. I haven't had any contact with him since someone tried to blow him up."

"Thank you for whatever you can do," Glass said, and headed for the door. With his hand on the knob he turned. "The day I was born is a black mark on the calendar of world history," he said, and went out.

I waited for Al to say something, but he didn't. He just sat there, gently massaging his eyes with the tips of his fingers.

"How's the charming Lillian this morning?" I asked.

He looked at me. "She's a wonderful girl, Hally. If this thing goes wrong, what the hell will I have to offer her? Mine will be the first head to roll in the basket, you know."

# TWO

When I walked out of the conference room at TAB, the receptionist handed me a folded message form.

"I was told not to disturb you, Mr. Hallam," she said. Like all the girl employees at TAB, this one could have been on the front chorus line of a Broadway musical.

The message was from Jericho. Would I join him at Zirato's for lunch when I got through my business at TAB?

The noonday traffic was heavy and the steady rain seemed to have reduced the number of available taxis to zero. It was four long cross-town blocks and another three downtown to Zirato's. I had to make it on shanks' mare.

Zirato's is a madhouse at lunch time. Everybody wants to be served at once, and somehow everyone is. Bernie was at the red velvet rope near the front door, telling all new arrivals that there would be a considerable wait. But he grinned at me and personally took my sopping raincoat

100

and hat.

"Booth in the right-hand rear corner," he said.

From today's perspective it was a strange luncheon. I thought Pat Barry looked a little beat. I thought Jericho looked properly grim for a man who'd been the target of a bomb. As I joined them, I knew nothing, of course, about Pat's story of her own private horror, nor did I know that her presence at the Mews had been any more than a coincidence.

"You could have called me sooner," I said, as I sat down next to Jericho, facing Pat across the table.

"There were things to do," Jericho said. His voice sounded ragged. I realized that neither he nor Pat could have had any sleep at all the night before. That accounted for their obvious frayed condition, I thought.

"Do I have to ask what the hell happened?" I said, when neither of them spoke.

Before Jericho could answer me, we were joined at the table by Lieutenant Pascal, the man from homicide. I realized that he, too, was answering a summons.

"Thanks for coming," Jericho said. He introduced the lieutenant to Pat. Pascal's smile was appreciative.

"Johnny may be able to paint what he sees, Miss Barry, but his description of you in words was inadequate." He sat down next to Pat. "From all accounts you two had yourself an evening."

"You've heard the details?" Jericho asked.

"On the ticker at headquarters and from Welch, your precinct captain."

"Then your information is incomplete," Jericho said.

"Oh, I'm certain of that," Pascal said, smiling. "Any time you tell a strange cop the whole truth about yourself, Johnny, that will be Columbus Day. Having seen you earlier in the morning—too damned early, I may say—I wondered about the rioting moppets."

"Someone phoned Pat from here—or at least supposedly from here—with a message from me. She was to come to the Mews. She did. She waited because I was at your place talking to you. When I arrived, we talked in the hall a minute and then—boom! If we'd gone straight in, they could have swept us up in a dustpan."

Pascal's smile was still there, but his gray eyes were cold.

"You don't know who phoned you?" he asked Pat.

She shook her head.

"Man?"

"Yes," she said. "He told me Johnny had just left here and asked him to phone. The voice was quiet, cultivated."

"Have you ever heard Don Ferrick speak?" Pascal asked.

"No."

"But if you heard the voice again—"

"I'd know it, if it was for real."

"How do you mean?"

"It was very precise, Lieutenant. It could have been 'put on'—which is the way my mother described acting. Acting was 'putting on.' We're dealing with show people, aren't we?"

"Brains, too," Pascal said. It was meant as a compliment for Pat.

"I choke on it a little," Jericho said. "If it weren't for the phone call to Pat, I'd buy the rioting kids. If it was Ferrick, he planned something with incredible speed. But getting Pat to the Mews—making her a joint target—well, you can't pin that on a mob of noisy kids who never heard of either of us."

"The police lab is checking out the pieces of the bomb your janitor swept up," Pascal said. "The results could help. You know why I'm here, Johnny?"

"Because I sent for you," Jericho said impatiently.

"Because I've never known you to ask for help before," Pascal said. "What is it you think I can do for you?"

"Pat's got to be protected," Jericho said. "I can't stand guard, waiting for Ferrick to move again. I'm not very clever with a catcher's mitt. I've got to move in on Ferrick."

"Maybe you're the one who needs protecting," Pascal said.

"Ferrick could use Pat to turn me helpless," Jericho said. "You might help by opening up the Nolan case again. He was murdered, Dave. Put the heat on in that direction and Ferrick may find himself too busy to bother about revenge."

"There's no basis for reopening the Nolan case. I may respect your judgment, but the department isn't going to assign men to poke sticks at a dead duck."

"Pat could stay at my place," I said. "I wouldn't mind standing guard."

"One of the first places they'd look," Jericho said. "You're my friend."

"I think I can solve that problem for a short time anyway," Pascal said. "You and Miss Barry are supposed to go to Welch's precinct house to make a formal statement, Johnny. Suppose I take you there from here in a police car. At the precinct house I can slide Miss Barry out a back door and take her to my apartment. She'll be perfectly safe there—if she'll stay put. That'll give us some time to nose around Ferrick and see just how hard he's looking for you."

"He's not going to have any trouble finding me," Jericho said. He gave a sharp little tug at his bright red beard. "I'm going to get myself a couple of hours' sleep, and then I'm going to save him the trouble of looking."

"We'll talk about that after Miss Barry is safe," Pascal said.

"There's nothing to talk about," Jericho said. "You don't buy Nolan's murder. Someone has to."

"You're very much on their minds," I said, and gave him a brief account of my session in the conference room at TAB.

"You can tell Mr. Glass for me that I won't withdraw as Pat's agent in the matter of Nolan's paintings," Jericho said. "You can also tell him for me I think he would be a wise man if he paid off whoever has to be paid off and forget the whole project of a Zelda Rankin special. Tell him

104

my crystal ball is dark with thunderclouds."

"Oh, you're not to be allowed to quit," I told him. "Perry Lewis loves you, presumably for knocking over his wife's boy friend. You quit and Zelda will suddenly come down with a condition called 'no voice.'"

"You should make a note, Hally, to write a book called 'The Complete Creep.'"

I noticed that Pascal was looking at Pat Barry, a puzzled little frown creasing his forehead. She seemed to be staring straight ahead into space.

"Is my place an agreeable solution for you, Miss Barry?" he asked.

She turned to him, the dark violet eyes blank. I thought she really must be beat. She hadn't been listening! . . .

When I was a small kid I was caught up in the wonderful world of pulp-magazine stories. I used to devour by the yard the works of people like Fred MacIsaac, Judson Philips, Erle Stanley Gardner, H. Bedford-Jones, and dozens of others. I remember there came a day when I asked myself a realistic question about the great pulp heroes. When did they sleep—or eat, or go to the bathroom? In the time schedule of those old stories there was literally no moment set aside for the necessities.

After lunch, which nobody seemed to eat, Pascal took us all to Captain Welch's precinct house in the village, where Jericho and Pat made formal statements for the record. This time, at Pascal's insistence, Welch was given all the facts. He didn't seem pleased at having been held

105

out on in the first place. A lot of time had passed in which he might have been trying to place Don Ferrick somewhere in the Village at the time of the bombing. I think he might have played it a lot tougher except for a private head-to-head with Pascal, who evidently carried plenty of weight with the captain.

While Jericho was answering some questions from the captain, Pascal swept Pat away without our realizing that she'd gone. Afterward I learned that he took her to his place and sent a policewoman to her apartment to pick up fresh clothes and some other necessities.

Finally Jericho came back to my apartment with me. I would be watchdog while he slept it out. On the way uptown in a taxi I knew, instinctively, that there was something he wasn't telling me. I hinted around and got nowhere. Something had him down, and he's rarely down when he's in action. I knew better than to press it too hard.

He was in bed about two o'clock and he slept like a poled ox until about eight in the evening. The minute he was awake he called Pascal's place. Pascal answered.

"She's still asleep," the lieutenant told Jericho.

"Anything on Ferrick's whereabouts at bomb time?" Jericho asked.

"Nothing. We haven't asked Zelda about him, because obviously Zelda will testify as promised."

"I'm moving in," Jericho said.

"How do you mean?"

"Pat and I can't wait around like sitting ducks for Ferrick to try again," Jericho said. "I'm moving in on Mr. Fancy. I'm going to force him to play his game on my time, not his."

"You can wind up behind half a dozen different eight balls," Pascal said. "I can't cover for you, Johnny, if you get yourself in big trouble."

"I don't ask for anything except that you take care of the girl."

"I can't force her to stay here if she decides to go somewhere else when she wakes up."

"Then charm her into staying," Jericho said.

"Play it cool, Johnny," Pascal said. "This crowd isn't predictable."

"Neither am I," Jericho said, his voice grim.

He ate almost all of a cold chicken I had in my refrigerator, along with half a loaf of Italian bread, spread with sweet butter. He washed it down with an iced coffee laced with a brandy that deserved a better fate. He seemed to brighten up considerably as he ate.

"There are questions we need answered, Hally," he said. He ticked them off on his huge, thick fingers. "First, where did the sleeping pills, or their equivalent, come from that killed Nolan? Did any of Zelda's crowd see Nolan's drink poisoned? Who followed us to Zirato's after the fracas at Zelda's last night? Whoever called Pat knew we were there. And finally, what did Ferrick do and where did he go when he came to after I slugged him?"

"There's one thing I've wondered about," I said.

"Try it out loud."

"We know Nolan was pretty tight when he left Zelda's two nights ago. The druggist supports that, and so does the taxi driver who had to help him get the front door of his apartment open. What we don't know, Johnny, is whether there was anyone waiting there for him. That's when it could have happened, you know. He was drunk. Some unknown chum sees the opportunity to finish him off and takes advantage of it. It could have had nothing whatever to do with Zelda's crowd."

"Are you suggesting Pat?" he asked in a flat voice.

"No. I simply suggest that we've made villains out of the people we'd like to be the villains."

"This unknown chum threw a bomb through my sky-light?"

"Of course not. That has to be Ferrick. But—"

"I have a single-track mind, Hally. The whole thing begins and ends for me with Zelda's crowd. I can smell it! In any case, I've got to get Ferrick off my back—mine and Pat's."

I shrugged. "So, where do we go from here?"

"You don't go anywhere," he said. "You stay here ready to grab that phone when and if it rings. If it's Pat, make sure she doesn't stir from Pascal's. If it's someone with a message from me, you'll know he's a liar. If it's me, you'll know I'm in bad trouble." . . .

Saturday night on the town means a lot of different things to a lot of different people. To the comfortably fixed couple in the three-and-a-half-room apartment on

108

West End Avenue it could be dinner at the House of Chan and two loge seats at the Radio City Music Hall where Julie Andrews is playing in something as sweet as can be. To the out-of-town buyer on a big expense account it can mean dinner at "21," scalper-priced tickets to a hit musical, and a ringside table at the Copa afterward. To the more sophisticated it can be one of the more inaccessible "rooms" at the Plaza or the Beaumont, with a big-name singing star to entertain and a heavy dose of alleged conversation. To the moppets in Greenwich Village it means having at it in the hallway of some cold-water tenement. To Jericho there are only two things worth thinking about on any night: work, or finding the place where the action is. The action must be predicated on a cause in which he's interested. It can take him anywhere from the Trapeze Bar at the Beaumont in New York, to a back-alley café in Hong Kong, to a front-line bloodletting in Vietnam, to a water-front saloon on the North River.

On this particular Saturday night Jericho's cause was justice for a dead painter, peace of mind for a tragic girl, and the permanent deactivating of a long-haired psycho. The scene of the early action was the Barber Pole Club on Second Avenue, not far from Zirato's. This Saturday was the final night of a month-long engagement at the Barber's for Zelda Rankin. Tomorrow she would, in theory, rest, and Monday she would go before the cameras in Brooklyn to make her special.

The Barber Pole Club has been called Las Vegas-on-the-East River. The girls are nearly all bare. The acts are varied, and there are periods of what is known as dancing —the frug, the Watusi, or whatever else is *in* at the moment. These dance intervals for the customers are, in some opinions, more entertaining than the professional acts. The strange gyrations, the non-touching sexuality of the dance routines, the two cages over the bar in which seminude young ladies jiggle their assets, create a kind of heated excitement. It's Jericho's theory that everyone wants to be a performer, to be watched. One of the easiest ways to get people to watch you is to undress. The girls in these public dance segments at the Barber's manage to reveal more than the professional strippers in the floor show.

Jericho headed for the Barber's when he left me that night. He wanted to see Zelda in action. He hit the gilded saloon in the middle of one of the raucous public dance moments. He had to fight his way to the long mahogany bar where a dozen bartenders worked overtime. What was going on sounded to him like a tribal war dance, with all the same hysterical excitement. He had to shout his order for a double bourbon on the rocks. He was bumped into and shoved and jostled. He was choked by the smells of tobacco and perfume and stale liquor and sweat. The red-and-white barber-pole motif of the décor was offensive to him. It occurred to him that he was the only person in the place not totally delighted by the goings-on. He found himself watching the five-piece combo that was pounding out the strange rhythms. They seemed swept away by their own magic, on the edge of some sort of orgiastic ful-

110

fillment.

And then it ended, amid groans and boos. The organized noise was replaced by a bedlam of shouting and screaming. The musicians left the bandstand, headed for a refill on whatever it was that kept them going. Jericho was about to try to make himself heard with a question to the nearest bartender on when Zelda was likely to appear again, when the lights in the place began to dim. Several sharp squeals of delight rose above the general din. The nearest bartender refilled Jericho's glass without being requested and then seemed to fade into the background. The room grew darker and darker, and then in front of the bandstand an overhead spot created a bright, circular cone of light.

Someone was on the bandstand again, and Jericho recognized Jimmy Cooper, Zelda's accompanist. The din faded into nothing. It was hard to believe, but there wasn't even the tinkle of ice in glasses.

Then, into the one bright shaft of light, Zelda came.

A soft but unharmonic chord was struck on the piano. Then Zelda began to sing, and with the first note a sigh swept over the audience, punctuated by one high-pitched little scream from the shadows.

Jericho hadn't paid much attention to Zelda at the Hell Hole the night before. His anger at the snake dance around the artistic remains of Tommy Nolan and his brief but violent encounter with Fancy Ferrick had kept him occupied.

"In action she's unbelievable," he told me later. "The

brief glimpse I'd had of her the night before had left me with the picture of a small slim girl, with her hair—or hair piece—piled high up on her head and incredibly long false eyelashes. A skinny nothing. But standing there in the single shaft of light, fires burned inside her. The voice is small and clear. You'd think she'd have to work in a small room, but you suddenly realize she could be heard in the top gallery at the opera. The sound is so clear, so perfect, so magnificently under control. The girl is a really great pro."

That was the highest compliment he could pay her. He couldn't tell me what she sang. The songs weren't familiar to him. They were her songs, written for her. The crowd knew them. As each one began, there was a mass moan of pleasure and then that unbelievable stillness, complete attention.

"She had on one of those plain white, hanging things," Jericho said. "I guess they call them the chemise. I've always thought they were godawful—no fit, no nothing. On this girl it was exciting. You seemed to be aware that nothing touched the quivering body underneath the dress. No jewelry, no accessories. No tricks with a handkerchief, or a fan, or a flower. She just stands there, her arms at her sides, her head raised a little, and sings, as if it was just for herself and no one else. For a moment I understood how Rich Ragsdale could have thought of Tommy Nolan's painting her face into his picture of the reaching girl. So help me, Hally, for a moment the idea didn't seem impossible to me. What she does with her songs about eager,

112

hungry, tragic youth is pure magic."

Standing with his back to the bar, Jericho felt a sudden sharp pain at his left wrist. He looked down and saw that someone was gripping him, bright scarlet nails biting into his flesh. They belonged to a girl, probably not more than sixteen, who was watching Zelda with shining eyes and parted lips. She wasn't aware that she had hold of Jericho. He could have been a gatepost.

Another astonishing thing was that there was no applause when she finished a song. Someone, probably an out-of-town buyer, started clapping at the end of the first number and was promptly hushed. She sang steadily for perhaps forty minutes. In all that time no one was served a drink at the Barber's, no waiter clattered a dish, no noisy drunk tried to project himself into the silence.

"It was almost like a religious ceremony," Jericho told me, "and so help me, Hally, I was caught up in it."

It ended like no other performance of its kind Jericho had ever seen. A song finished on a high clear note, held in a swelling and then tapering moment of almost perfect sound. Then the shaft of light disappeared. A second later the main house lights came up and Zelda was gone.

The place went wild, stampings, yellings, screamings, and a thunder of applause that couldn't be stopped. The pain was gone from Jericho's wrist and he saw that the girl had turned away, her eyes brimming with tears. The bartenders were at work; the waiters scampered, and the audience stood and shouted for Zelda. It was evidently not part of her routine to return for bows. They knew it,

113

and they tried to make her hear their appreciation through the brick walls of the building.

Someone tapped Jericho on the shoulder and he turned. The bartender was holding a slip of paper out to him. He made a gesture that indicated it was impossible for him to be heard over the explosion of noise in the place. On the back of a bar tab was written: "Miss Rankin would like you to come to her dressing room."

The bartender pointed to a small door back of the bandstand, which was suddenly reoccupied by the combo. The customers were going to have a chance to release their pent-up emotions with another session of a-go-go. The trumpeter, his eyes closed, sent a blast of brassy sound into the thick air, and the place was jumping again.

Jericho edged his way past the stand and through the door that led to the dressing rooms.

The glamour was gone here. The brick walls were scrawled with lewd drawings and juvenile smut. A man in a clown's make-up, evidently part of the act to go on next, asked if he could do something for Jericho and directed him to the door of Zelda's dressing room at the end of the hall. Jericho knocked and heard her clear voice inviting him in.

She was sitting at a dressing table, facing a mirror that was ringed by colored lights. The white dress she'd worn on stage hung inside a plastic bag on a pole that crossed a corner of the room. There were half a dozen other dresses that seemed to be exact duplicates. The simple white

114

chemise was evidently Zelda's performing uniform.

She was wearing a pink smock with a few make-up stains on it. She studied herself closely in the mirror as she took off some of the heavy theatrical eye make-up with cream and tissue. She didn't turn to look at him because she could see him in the mirror too.

"Thanks for coming," she said. "I saw you at the bar."

"I've never heard you before," he said. "I only know now what I've missed. It's wonderfully good, Zelda."

Close up, she surprised him. He knew she was no child. He knew of her strange sado-masochistic relationship with her husband. He knew of the rumored love affair with Don Ferrick. You would expect a kind of tough worldliness to be revealed off stage. There were tiny lines at the corners of her eyes and on either side of her slightly trembling mouth, but the eager, wounded little girl was still there.

"I'm flattered to have you think so," she said. "I know you're not someone to pass meaningless compliments."

"Excellence moves me," Jericho said. "I understand now why your doing this television special is so important to so many people. I know why the advertiser doesn't want anyone else."

She stared at his reflection in the mirror. There was a quality of pleading in her wide eyes. "Help me to do it," she said.

"I don't follow," he said.

"You have charge of Nolan's paintings," she said. "Don't be sticky with Rich Ragsdale. Those paintings send me,

Jericho. I think they'll help me give a show no one will forget."

"I'm glad I came here tonight," he said. "Any notions I had that you might be exploiting Nolan's great talent to promote something cheap are gone. I should have known he wouldn't have agreed to let you use them unless he'd felt you had as much to offer in your way as he had in his."

"I wasn't worried about that," she said. "And you mustn't worry about Ragsdale. He's really marvelous at his job. I need your help in quite another way."

"Oh?"

"Let Don Ferrick alone," she said, her eyes suddenly lowered.

Jericho's smile was bright and hard. "Shouldn't I be asking you to ask him to let me alone? I'm the one who was bombed out, Zelda."

"He didn't do it," she said without conviction.

"I've heard you'll testify to that effect," he said, the friendliness gone from his voice.

She suddenly brought both clenched fists down on the dressing table so hard that bottles and jars bounced. "A person only has so much energy," she said. "It takes an enormous amount of it to perform. I think you know that. Then I must deal round the clock with Perry, never knowing ahead of time just what his mood will be, or his demands. And then I have to deal with Don."

"Have to?" he asked.

"Have you never been hooked by anything?" she asked.

116

It had a desperation in it. "Liquor, or food, or women, or something? I can't help myself, Jericho. I tell myself ten times a day that I'll leave Perry, that I'll run away from his cruelties and his endless foibles. I can't. I tell myself I'll never let Don touch me again, but then he does—just the caress of his fingers on my cheek—and I'm lost. I have to give him whatever he wants. If I think he may not come back some day, I begin to die inside. If I think he's in danger, I can't think of anything else. Please, I beg you, Jericho, let him alone at least until after the special is finished. If I have to worry about him, I'll never get through it."

"I can't promise anything," Jericho said. "Your fancy friend tried to kill me awhile ago, and he tried to kill a completely innocent girl, and I mean to have his hide for it, Zelda. You can swear till you're blue in the face that he was with you and that he couldn't have tossed that bomb through my studio skylight, and I won't believe you. There's even less chance of my believing you now that you've told me how things are."

"What's your price?" she asked in a small, pinched voice.

"No price," he said, angry at her for asking.

"I can keep Don away from you if you'll keep away from him," she said.

"No deal."

She turned around on the stool and stood up. The pink smock hung loose and unfastened. "From now until ten o'clock on Monday morning when I have to start filming

117

the special I have no obligations," she said. "Would that much time with me persuade you to forget about Don?"

His smile was bitter. "Best offer I've had since my sophomore year in prep school," he said. "I'll bet you're awfully good at it too. But regretfully it's not my price."

A little shudder ran over the body underneath the smock. "Damn you!" she whispered.

Jericho told me later that he felt a little ashamed of himself. She had offered the only thing she had which she thought might appeal to him. It had taken a kind of twisted courage.

"I think you may not be up to date on the facts of life," he said quietly. "It isn't just a feud with Ferrick that concerns me, Zelda. I don't believe for an instant that Tommy Nolan committed suicide."

"But—"

"I think somebody poisoned his drink, or drinks, at your place that night and that he just did get home to die."

"No!" A hand went up to her trembling lips.

"There's a murderer in the mad, mad world of Zelda Rankin, baby, and I mean to point a finger at him—or her."

"No!" she cried out. "You're wrong! We all liked Tommy, even if we did argue with him like cats and dogs! I liked him and admired him. Rich thought he was the greatest! He got to Don, because Don, in a way, is the end result of the crazy world Tommy was painting. Nobody I know wanted Tommy dead. So help me."

"There are others," Jericho said. "The network people,

118

the product people, the music people."

"There's no one!" she protested.

His eyes narrowed. "Maybe I will make you a deal," he said. "There'll be the usual brawl back at the Hell Hole tonight?"

She nodded. "Party—to celebrate my closing here and the special coming up. All kinds of people."

"Take me with you," Jericho said. "Let me listen and look for myself. If you can convince me—"

"Don will be there," she said sharply.

"I counted on it, baby. But he's not likely to kill me in public, or I him. If you can convince me that nothing happened to Tommy Nolan at your place—"

"Wait for me outside," Zelda interrupted. "I'll be dressed in five minutes. You'll see how wrong you are, Jericho."

# Three

One of the main problems of the evening was to get Zelda from the stage door of the Barber Pole Club to the big black limousine that waited for her at the curb. There was a chauffeur in a neat black uniform who looked as though he'd been recruited from the National Football League, but it took all he and Jericho had combined to get Zelda through the mob of teen-agers who were waiting for her to appear. The analogy with a kind of religious frenzy came back to Jericho. A couple of hundred kids wanted to touch her, as if the simple contact would cure their own anguish. They weren't autograph hounds; they were worshipers.

Jericho felt as though he'd been in a free-for-all when he finally found himself in the back seat of the limousine with that strange, hypnotic girl. She sat pressed in one corner of the seat, as far away from him as she could get. The

120

drive to the Hell Hole was a short one, and she didn't speak once on the way. When they arrived at the three brownstone houses, Jericho saw that the mob scene would have to be repeated. Kids evidently knew that she came straight home after the show at the Barber's, and they were waiting for her.

Jericho and the chauffeur put together a kind of flying wedge with Zelda between them and got her to the front door. There she turned, standing straight and still in another of those unfitted chemises, hanging just to her knees, this one a pale yellow. The noisy mob was suddenly, totally silent.

"Good night, my darlings," Zelda said.

They ducked through the front door, and as it closed, a roar of hysterical approval rose behind them. Zelda leaned against the wall of the entrance hall, her eyes closed, as if the experience had exhausted her. From upstairs came the sound of the piano and the beat of Jimmy Cooper's foot on the floor and a babel of voices. The party here was started.

Zelda opened her eyes. "Do me one favor, Jericho. Wait here for five minutes! Eddie will get you a drink if you want one." She nodded toward the grinning chauffeur.

"You're spoiling my evening," Jericho said. "I counted on seeing Ferrick's face when he unexpectedly saw me arrive."

"Please!"

"Your party," Jericho said.

She hurried away up the stairs. Eddie, the chauffeur,

watched her go.

"Some doll," he said. "Thanks for the help. Some nights I think I won't make it. It was going to be bad tonight because they all know this was her last public appearance for a while."

"She's certainly got those kids wrapped around her finger."

"Totalsville," Eddie said. "Drink?"

"I can wait."

"Why wait? In a little while they'll be three deep at the bar up there. This is mob-scene night all over."

"A shot of bourbon on the rocks," Jericho said.

Eddie opened a sliding door which revealed a complete small service bar. "The boss would like to have one of these on every landing," Eddie said.

"Perry Lewis?"

Eddie nodded as he put ice in a glass. "He's scared of getting caught between floors without a slug of something."

"Alcoholic?"

"You need a genius to answer that," Eddie said. "When he wants to stay sober, he can drink a gallon and not bat an eyelash. Other times two drinks will have him weaving." He handed Jericho his drink. "Have a happy," he said.

Jericho was aware that Eddie was studying him with a kind of shrewd, city-boy look. "Can't help hearing the talk about last night," he said. His smile was crooked. "There's quite a few of us got a kick out of hearing that Ferrick

122

squared off against something a little too tough for him."

"You look as though you could handle yourself," Jericho said.

"When you play with Ferrick and his boys, you play for all the marbles," Eddie said. "I figured you ought to know that."

"If you've heard the news on radio and TV about what happened to my studio early this morning, you'll know that I do know."

Eddie nodded. "I figured it might be him," he said.

"Where does he hang out, Eddie, when he's not here?"

Eddie shrugged. "He never rides with me unless Zelda is with him. I understand there's a kind of a club somewhere on the upper East Side. The members all wear their hair long and dress in those cuckie clothes. Ferrick's always bringing some of them here. I figure this club is where he stays when he isn't here." The pug face hardened. "It's funny the guys women go for. Most of us worship Zelda, and I'm not talking about those kids out on the street. She could have my right arm if she asked for it. There's thousands of decent guys would take care of her and love her. And what does she do?" He glanced up the stairs toward the party noise. "She makes herself the joint property of the two biggest creeps of all time. Hard to figure."

Jericho sipped his drink. Eddie's kind of gossip could be helpful. "You run across the young painter fellow who is supposed to have killed himself a couple of nights ago?"

"Supposed to?" Eddie asked, his eyes bright.

"I don't think he did. I think somebody slipped him a Mickey, right here in this house."

Eddie whistled softly. "Boy, do I wish I could pin it on Ferrick. Or even the boss!"

"What did they or anyone else have against Nolan?"

Eddie shook his head slowly. "You can't figure things around here the way you'd figure them anywhere else," he said. "I punch a guy in the nose and you know he's been groping around my chick, or stealing from me, or trying to get me in trouble I don't deserve. But here? Brother! Ferrick might kill a guy for laughing at the cut of his frock coat. The boss would spend months figuring a way to destroy a guy, business-wise, because the guy didn't recognize that Mr. Perry Lewis is King of Show Business. Some of the rest of these people might kill you just because they soaked a sugar cube in LSD and went off their rocker—for no reason at all except kicks. They don't play by any rules here, mister. It's no place for a nice kind of a nut like you—or that Nolan guy, for that matter. They all seemed to like him. They argued and shouted at each other, but I had the feeling Nolan was appreciated as an okay kid."

Jericho looked at his watch. "Well, I guess my five minutes is up, Eddie. Thanks for the local color."

"Any time," Eddie said. "Keep your eye on your rearview mirror, if you see what I mean."

Jericho walked up the stairs to the huge second-floor party room. There were ten or fifteen people scattered around the room. The main party crowd was still to come. Perry Lewis, wearing a bright gold summer dinner jacket,

124

was working behind the bar. Jimmy Cooper, the inevitable frayed cigar gripped between his teeth, was working his particular magic at the piano, surrounded by a half-dozen suckers for real Dixieland, including the two girls from the night before in their transparent evening gowns. They were probably different gowns, but how you tell one transparency from another Jericho didn't know.

Jericho's arrival wasn't unexpected. Across the room he saw Don Ferrick, tall and elegant in a pale-blue period frock coat, a high, flowered collar and cravat, tight-fitting houndstooth check trousers, a frilly shirt, and beautifully made, shiny black cowboy-type evening boots. Ferrick's face was dead white with anger. Zelda was clinging to his arm as if she hoped to hold him back by sheer weight. Standing at one end of the bar, close together, were two young men, duplicating Ferrick's hair style and general dress pattern. They looked quickly from Ferrick to Jericho and back again. It was fairly obvious that, if there was to be trouble, Jericho would have more than Ferrick to handle. In a far corner of the room Al Stover sat on a small sofa with Lillian Heller close to him. They both gave him tense little waves of greeting. Mike Crowley and Martin Farmer, the two P.R. men, were there, looking happily tight but watchful. The whole gathering seemed to be aware that an explosion was in the balance—a very delicate balance.

Perry Lewis broke the general tension by shouting over the sound of Jimmy Cooper's piano. "Hey, pal! Over here! Drink on the management."

Out of the corner of his eye Jericho saw Ferrick turn abruptly away and walk out of the room at the far end, Zelda still with him, talking to him earnestly. Jericho eased over to the bar where Perry was already pouring a slug of bourbon.

"Welcome, oh knight in shining armor," he said. "I halfway expected you wouldn't show, in spite of what I know about you."

"What do you know about me besides that I drink bourbon—and how did you know that?"

"Called the bartender at the Players," Perry said. "I'm even up to date on this." He produced a lime from behind the bar and sliced it in half with a surgical-bladed knife. "I figured Zelda might lure you away to save her Donny boy's hide. Tell me, did she try, and didn't you find her attractive enough?" The dark eyes were burning with a queer eagerness.

Jericho's bearded face was a mask. "She didn't try," he said quietly.

"Oh, come now, Michelangelo," Perry said. From under the bar he produced a small tape recorder. "Part of my pleasure in life is to know everything Zelda does, everything she feels, every moment of ecstasy and pain."

The tape began to turn, and Jericho heard Zelda's voice: "From now until ten o'clock on Monday morning when I have to start filming the special I have no obligations. Would that much time with me persuade you to forget about Don?"

And Jericho's voice: "Best offer I've had since my

*sophomore year in prep school. I'll bet you're awfully good at it too. But—"*

Jericho's massive fist came down on the tiny tape recorder and smashed it flat. He was smiling, but it was a smile that should have frightened Perry.

"No hard feelings, Johnny boy," Perry said, and swept the shattered recorder off the bar and out of sight. "I buy them by the gross, and where Zelda goeth, they goeth."

"Someone referred to you as a prize jerk," Jericho said. "The description doesn't do you justice."

" 'Sticks and stones can break my bones, but names . . . ' et cetera, et cetera. Don't you know that you're my hero of the moment, Johnny boy? You afforded me what may be my only chance to see Don boy shown up for an overinflated phony. His little boy friends over there cried and cried after you left. And didn't your friend, Hallam, tell you my ultimatum to the great TV brain? Jericho stays or no show. They had to buy it, pal. It doesn't say so anywhere in print, but I am the queen-maker and the king-breaker around these parts. You are to be the late Thomas Nolan's protector, and that's that."

Perry was clearly on the way to one of his quick drunks which Eddie, the chauffeur, had described.

"Our mutual chum, Al Stover, tells me you have fantastic theories about Tommy's passing. A deadly Finn, fed to him by one of our beloved friends. Oh, come, Daddio!"

Jericho picked up his drink. "Tell me about that last time Nolan was here," he said.

Perry's eyes narrowed to shiny black shoe buttons. The

127

conversation was quite private, because Jimmy Cooper's piano shut out the chance of its being overheard unless someone crowded in to join them. He took a wide-mouthed thermos from under the bar and began to fill it with shaved ice. He was apparently going to retire to his divan and his pass-out early.

"Little Tommy Nolan was quite a kid," Perry said. "I'm one of the popular front who knows nothing about art but I-know-what-I-like-department. Tommy probably wasn't any good, because I liked what he painted. It sends me. Which is probably the artistic kiss of death. Anyway, Tommy was well liked—to quote Willy Loman. We kidded and argued and fought, but he was well liked. Nobody mickeyed him around here, Johnny boy."

"Did he often get drunk the way he did that night?"

Perry laughed. "Special occasion," he said. "Rich Ragsdale had been teasing him about painting Zelda's face into one of his pictures. He was only kidding, but on the subject of his work Tommy couldn't take a joke. He had a great sense of humor about everything except his own bloody work. It was a night for needling him, but I promise you, Johnny boy, it wasn't anything that would have driven him off his rocker. He was a pretty damn well oriented kid."

"Which is why I don't think he killed himself."

"Maybe he was experimenting. That's one of the big deals with the kids today. They experiment with sex and liquor and drugs and what have you." Perry chuckled. "That night he was showing off, you might say experi-

128

menting."

"How do you mean?"

Perry indicated the thermos jug he was filling with ice. "Usually someone else prepares this for me," he said. "Zelda, or Don boy, or Marty Farmer, or some of the crowd. It's the same thing every night. Scotch on shaved ice. This mug holds a fifth. That night—Tommy's last night—we'd gotten into a shouting comic-opera argument. I can do everything better than you can! I was lying on that divan over there and Tommy was bending over me, saying he was better at thinking, eating, love-making, and anything else I cared to name. It happened that just at that moment someone handed me my thermos of scotch. 'And drink better!' Tommy shouted at me. He grabbed the thermos, and so help me, he drank the whole thing without once taking it away from his mouth. 'Try that on your pianola sometime!' he said, and went barging out of here, high as a kite. So I figure he got home, really stoned, and did some experimenting with pills—or took 'em by mistake."

Jericho's pale-blue eyes were fixed on Perry as if he was hypnotized. And then he threw back his head and roared with laughter.

"What's so funny?" Perry asked, frowning. Jericho's laughter was a thunder of sound, but it wasn't, somehow, contagious.

Jericho put his empty glass down on the bar. "The thing that's bugged me from the start about this is that I couldn't figure why even you creeps should want Nolan out of the way. I could swear he didn't commit suicide or experiment with drugs and kill himself. But I couldn't figure why any of you would kill him. Don't you see, Mr. King-Breaker, we finally know what happened to Tommy. It was an accident. The person who was meant to die that night was you! Your jug was loaded. Your jug had the Mickey in it, and you were meant to drink it. And then, right in front of the murderer's eyes, Nolan grabbed the jug out of your hands and drank it instead of you."

Perry Lewis stared at the thermos as if it were a poison snake. Then he began to shout at the top of his lungs:

"All of you! Be quiet. I've got to think!"

His face was the color of ashes, and it was covered with a thin film of sweat. He moistened his lips, and then he lifted his eyes to look at Jericho.

"You could be right," he said. "You must be right."

"Who filled your thermos for you that night?"

Perry began to tremble from head to foot. "That we'll know before this night is over." He looked around at the roomful of startled faces.

"God damn the lot of you!" he shouted.

# Part 3

# One

Of course, it was complete guesswork. There wasn't a shred of proof, and no likelihood that there ever would be. The thermos had been used—washed and used—four or five times since it had contained a lethal dose. If it had contained one. The poisoner had been given five full days to remove all possible connection between himself and the fatal drink of scotch.

But everything fitted perfectly. The question had been raised as to how Tommy could accidentally have swallowed a Mickey without tasting the heavy dose of barbiturates. It was answered. He'd been putting on an act. If the drink tasted foul, he wouldn't have paid any attention. His intention was to empty the jug, no matter how distasteful or unpleasant the process. Then, being a rational human being, he'd realized he was going to feel like hell the following morning and had stopped at the drugstore for a bottle of bromo. The taxi driver had had to help him open the front door of his apartment building—not only because he was drunk, but because the drug was beginning to take effect. He'd managed to get into his apartment, undress, and tumble into bed. And then he must have realized that something more than sheer drunkenness had overtaken him. He'd staggered toward the phone and not made it. He'd died alone and probably unaware that it was the end for him.

Meanwhile, here at the Hell Hole, the poisoner must have been sweating blood when he saw Tommy drain the thermos. He couldn't warn him; he couldn't stop him without revealing his involvement. He'd killed the wrong man and he had to let it happen.

The puzzle over what possible motive there could have been for murder was resolved. Everyone connected with Perry Lewis had a motive, open or secret.

Jericho leaned on the bar, watching Perry's gray, working face. It must have been an incredible moment for this warped, bitter little sadist. The tables were turned on him. He was the target for a change, and except for the sheerest accident, he would at this moment be ashes instead of flesh and blood. Jericho saw terror in the narrowed black eyes and also a rage so violent that it rattled Perry's teeth together. He moved slowly out around the end of the bar. For the first time Jericho was aware of the limp Perry's crippled foot imposed on him. Perry stopped next to Jericho, wiping the saliva from the corners of his mouth with a white linen handkerchief. One of the girls in

134

the nude evening dresses giggled. She must have thought some kind of new, twisted joke was about to be put in motion. Somehow that inane little giggle broke the spell. Jimmy Cooper began to play "Yes, sir, she's my baby." Outbreaks by Perry evidently weren't unusual in the Hell Hole.

"Look at them," Perry said in a harsh whisper. He reached out a hand to Jericho's arm to steady himself. "Every night they come here to eat off me, to drink off me, to laugh at me, to watch Zelda at play. And one of them, by God—" He shook his head as if he couldn't believe it.

"Sometimes you can turn the screws too tight," Jericho said.

Blazing dark eyes looked up. "What do you mean?"

"I know your type, Perry. Needle, needle, needle until something gives—just for the hell of it. It seems the wrong guy paid off, but you should have an interesting time guessing where it's coming from the next time."

"You'll help me," Perry said.

Jericho's laugh was short. "Why the hell should I?"

"Because you want to clear up Tommy Nolan's name, don't you? And because you've got to settle with Don boy if you want to have any peace yourself."

"I'll settle with Don boy," Jericho said.

"Maybe I could help you in return for help," Perry said. "Some people gain power because they are magnetic and attractive. Some people who are bastards have it because they are brilliant at their jobs. Some people have power because they deal in other people's secrets. This, Johnny

135

boy, is the age of the bug, the hidden tape recorder, the electronic eye. I have a box of goodies that could smash everybody in this room—and some others who aren't here. I could bring Don boy crawling to you on his knees if I wanted to."

"I'll handle him," Jericho said.

"Not till I've handled him first," Perry said. "If you were trying to guess who the two people are who might most want me out of the way, who would you pick?"

"The list is so long," Jericho said dryly.

"I'll tell you who," Perry said, his voice shaken by a new spasm of fury. "Don boy and my beloved Zelda. My little machines have reported to me; my mechanical eyes have watched. No, first I deal with Don boy, and then you can have what's left. And just for kicks, everyone else in this mob of chiselers is going to learn a lesson from me. Do we have a deal? You help me, I help you?"

"We do not," Jericho said.

"Sorry, Johnny boy, because I like you—and I owe you for opening my eyes. But stay out of the way when the roof caves in, because it'll come down hard when it does."

"Had you thought of calling in the police?" Jericho asked. "Murder's their job, and there was a murder, Perry."

"And wait six months for them to turn up something, wondering each morning whether it's safe to drink my coffee? No, baby, this one I settle for myself." His smile was like a knife edge. He'd recovered from the initial shock and he was his own man again, vicious and venge-

136

ful. "I begin by finding the lovebirds and telling them what the score is." He limped slowly away across the room.

There was a nightmarish quality to the entire moment. Faces looked enlarged to Jericho and out of focus. Voices were harsh. The piano sounds were pounded out in endless discords. There weren't any people like this anywhere, Jericho told himself. And yet here they were.

"You wouldn't know a way to persuade Perry to take a week's vacation, would you?" a voice drawled at Jericho's shoulder. "He seems to like you."

Rich Ragsdale was watching Perry limp through the door at the far end of the room. He was wearing the faded-blue denims, the turtle-necked knitted sports shirt, the faded seersucker jacket. A cigarette bobbed between his lips as he spoke. The weary, cynical eyes were buried behind the dark pouches in which they lived.

"I imagine that to ask him anything is to be refused," Jericho said.

"What was that explosion all about?" Ragsdale asked.

"He just figured out, with my help, that Nolan's death was a mistake. The poison was in Perry's thermos jug and was meant for him."

Ragsdale's expression didn't alter by so much as the blink of an eyelash. "I've been praying he wouldn't figure that one out until after we'd finished shooting the special," he said.

"You knew?" Jericho said, making no attempt to hide his surprise.

"What else?" Ragsdale said wearily. "Nobody had it in for Tommy. When I heard the news on the radio the next day, I remembered that scene with the thermos."

"It didn't occur to you to mention it to the police?"

"Not for a second," Ragsdale said calmly. "By then the jug had been scrubbed clean. The poisoner had got rid of his bottle or box or whatever he carried the stuff in. There was a hundred G's involved for me, and it happens I need it. Maybe if it would have done any good, I might have said something. Maybe. But I was guessing, just the way you're guessing. Telling the police isn't going to do anything except hurt a lot of people who've already been hurt too much and too often by Perry. I'm sorry you found it necessary to wise up Perry, because he'll lash out now like a dying octopus."

"Who else knows?" Jericho asked.

Ragsdale shrugged. "Whoever loaded the thermos jug with sleep dust."

"Any ideas?"

Ragsdale snorted. "Twenty or thirty," he said. He sobered. "I have to start rolling cameras in less than thirty-six hours. I think perhaps we ought to talk to Al Stover. He has a kind of genius for dealing with Perry in crisis. I have a hunch I'm going to need all his skills."

Al Stover, for whom so much was at stake in the matter of the special, was on his way across the room toward them, Lillian Heller on his arm, as Ragsdale spoke.

"What was all that?" he asked.

"Our Perry has discovered that he's not loved," Rags-

138

dale said. He gave Al and his girl a quick outline of what had set Perry off. Al listened, not believing.

"You knew all along about the thermos jug, Rich?"

"I guessed—as Jericho did," Rich said. "Only I saw it happen."

"And you let Tommy Nolan go without telling him?" Lillian Heller asked, in a kind of shock.

"My dear girl, I didn't know what I was seeing until the next morning when I heard about Nolan. The problem now is to keep Perry from making such a loud squawk or retaliating in some fashion that'll really put us out of business."

"Oh, God!" Al said.

"Chin up," Ragsdale said, a note of contempt in his voice. It was clear he wasn't Al Stover's number-one admirer. "I'd trot off and find Perry if I were you, Al. I'd make it clear to him how horrified we all are at the suggestion that someone tried to kill him. I'd assure him that we're all ready to lay down our lives to protect him." His chuckle was sardonic. "But mostly I'd mention money to him. I'd mention a quarter of a million bucks to him, over and over. I'd imply that until after the special is shot and shown he could lose a hell of a lot of bread and butter— plus jam—if he plays a big scene."

"You can ask Al to crawl too much, Mr. Ragsdale," Lillian said.

Ragsdale's heavy lids lowered. "I like a girl who will stand up for her man's manhood," he drawled. "But too many of us have too much at stake, honey, for Al to

139

choose this moment to remember what his psychiatrist told him about being an adult. We're playing with sick children and we have to act like sick children to stay in the game."

Al had no doubts. He seemed to get his second wind. "Make a couple of calls for me, Lillian," he said. "Get Nick Glass and tell him what's up. Marty Farmer and I will try to quiet Perry down." He looked at Jericho. "For God's sake, try not to start something else, will you, pal?"

"There won't be any serious trouble if you keep mentioning money, money, money," Ragsdale muttered. "I think I know my Perry."

"You could be wrong," Jericho said to the director, as Al and Lillian Heller took off. "He was badly scared. It could make him a lot more dangerous."

"Let us pray," Ragsdale said, and reached for a brandy bottle on the bar.

Jericho looked around the room, and he told me later he felt just a little sick at his stomach. Of course, they didn't know what had happened, these people—the two half-naked girls with their long-haired male dancing partners, bobbing and weaving to Jimmy Cooper's steady beat, never touching each other, but staring at each other with a kind of fascinated excitement. The two P.R. men had gone off with Al and Miss Heller. There was something unpleasantly decadent about the dancing foursome. Somewhere else a snake-bitten Perry was confronting Zelda and her lover. You had the feeling, Jericho told me, that the whole place would suddenly collapse of its own rot.

140

"You are being summoned," Ragsdale said softly, at Jericho's elbow.

Jericho turned and saw Zelda standing in the far doorway. She looked, at that distance, like a child in her straight-hanging yellow dress. She beckoned to Jericho.

"A dying request," Ragsdale murmured. "Stay out of that bed until after the special."

Jericho gave him a bright, hard look. "Does anything in the world matter to you except what happens on that idiot box of yours?"

"Nothing whatever," Ragsdale said with a sleepy smile.

Jericho walked across the room to where Zelda waited. He was aware that the dancers were suddenly watching him and not each other. Jimmy Cooper, chewing his cigar, gave Jericho a friendly grin, nodding to himself. Apparently things were going exactly as Jimmy had predicted.

Zelda reached out ice-cold fingers to Jericho almost before he reached her. Her eyes were wide, bright, the pupils enlarged. Jericho wondered if excitement alone could produce that result.

"You found out what you came to find out," she said in a tense whisper.

"Some of it," he said.

"So please go!" she said.

"Where's your friend Ferrick?"

Her body writhed under the yellow dress. "There's enough hell to pay here for one night without adding that. You and Don can settle things at some other time in some other place."

141

"I don't think I want to wait," he said, looking past her into a dimly lit hallway. He could hear Perry's voice, loud and angry, and Al Stover's, soft and pleading.

Tears welled up into Zelda's eyes. "I can't handle them both at the same time," she said. "Please, give me a chance. You can't blame Perry for blowing his top. He needs me. He needs Don."

"Needs Don?" Jericho said, eyebrows raised.

"Don's his bodyguard," she said, as though it was something everyone knew. "Perry can't have him distracted now that he's in trouble."

"I'll be damned," Jericho said. "I had your fancy friend marked down as a number-one suspect. I suppose there could be a stranger situation."

"Please give us a chance to live the next few days without any more trouble," Zelda pleaded. "I—I have a show to do. Don't you understand?"

"Perhaps I never will," Jericho said.

Her hands slid up his arms toward his shoulders. "Please, Jericho, let us work this out for ourselves. Afterward, if you and Don have to settle a score—"

"Don't you care to find out who tried to poison your husband?" Jericho asked

"Let *us* work it out!" she pleaded.

There was some kind of fresh commotion behind them, and Jericho turned. To his astonishment he saw that the new arrivals at the party were Lieutenant Pascal of Homicide and three other men in business suits who had cop written all over them. Pascal had a large piece of adhesive tape plastered over his right temple. His face was unnaturally pale, and his eyes were cold as two newly minted dimes. He spotted Jericho and came directly across the room to him. Zelda might as well not have been there.

"I'm sorry, Johnny," he said, his voice harsh.

"What the hell happened to you?" Jericho asked. Close up, he could see that Pascal's head was swollen around the adhesive-tape patch.

"There were seven or eight of them," Pascal said. "They blasted their way into my apartment."

"Blasted?"

"Blew the lock off with some kind of explosive," the detective said. "I was asleep. I didn't have a chance, Johnny. They were all over me."

"Pat?" Jericho asked sharply.

"That's what I'm sorry about," Pascal said. "When I came to, she was gone."

"You get a look at them?"

Pascal turned. He made a small angry gesture at the two long-haired male dancers. "That breed," he said. "I came here looking for your friend Ferrick—just in case."

Jericho turned on Zelda. She was leaning against the doorjamb for support. "Where is he?" Jericho demanded.

She moistened her lips. "The other house—" She waved down the dark passage. "My apartment—second floor at the back. But he's been here all evening!"

Pascal signaled to his men. "Question those two," he said. "Meehan, come with us."

"How long ago did this happen, Dave?" Jericho asked.

143

"Forty-five minutes—an hour."

"Those two have been here right along," Jericho said. "Ferrick was here when I arrived about that long ago."

"I'll show you where he is," Zelda said in an uncertain whisper. "He couldn't have had anything to do with—"

"Just take us to him, please," Pascal said in a frozen voice.

The dark hallway led into the adjoining house. It was like walking into another world. This was Zelda's playground. The colors were pastels. Jericho had the feeling that he was being taken into a little girl's nursery. At the end of a hallway was a sort of combination sitting room-dressing room. There was a chaise longue, fragile-looking chairs and tables, a full-length mirror in the back of a door that led either to a bedroom or bath, and literally hundreds of small toy animals. There was the entire cast of *Winnie-the-Pooh*, tiny rabbits, dogs, squirrels, almost any small creature you could imagine, many of them with wide pale ribbons tied around their necks. A large over-stuffed couch with a pale-yellow cover and cushions was so crowded with these little button-eyed toys that there was no place for a person to sit.

Standing in front of the full-length mirror, carefully adjusting his flowered cravat, was the tall, broad-shouldered figure of Don Ferrick. He turned, giving a little settling tug to his pale-blue frock coat, as though he'd just put it on. He ignored Zelda. He ignored Pascal and the plainclothes man behind him. His eyes fixed on Jericho.

"You don't ever give up, do you?" he said softly.

"I'm sorry, Don," Zelda said. "They insisted. I—"

"Just go away somewhere, baby," Don said, not taking his eyes off Jericho.

"You'll stay where you are, please, Mrs. Lewis," Pascal said. It was probably one of the few times Zelda had ever been called by her legal name.

Ferrick's eyes flickered toward Pascal. "Who are you to be giving orders around here?"

Pascal took the little leather-covered case that held his badge out of his pocket and flipped it open.

Ferrick looked back at Jericho with a small, contemptuous smile. "So you had to send for help," he said.

"Hold it, Johnny," Pascal said sharply, as Jericho took a step toward the dandified Ferrick. "How long have you been here this evening, Ferrick?"

"I wonder if I have to answer," Ferrick said. "I mean, legally. Well, there's no point in making an issue of it. I've been here all evening. It's my job."

"Job?"

"I look out for Perry Lewis," Ferrick said. A smile twitched the corners of his mouth. "I take care of him and everything that belongs to him."

"The last hour?" Pascal asked.

"Here," Ferrick said.

"You were here last night, I suppose, when Jericho's studio was bombed?"

Ferrick's eyes touched Zelda. "Oh, very much here," he said.

"About an hour ago a group of—of your counterparts,"

Pascal said, "broke into my apartment, beat me up, and took away a girl who was staying there under my protection. You know her, Ferrick. She is Patricia Barry."

"She leads an adventurous life," Ferrick said. "Last night a bomb when she was with Jericho, tonight an army of eager young men when she's with you. She goes for the rugged type, it seems, but without much luck."

"I suggest the characters who broke into my place were your friends," Pascal said. "I suggest this is all part of a private war you're having with Jericho. And I tell you that if Miss Barry isn't safely back in my hands within an hour, the heat that will be put on you will be memorable."

Ferrick looked at Pascal and laughed. "The name of the game is guessarama," he said. "In color, on a wide, wide screen."

Jericho spoke, so quietly it didn't sound like him. "There's one important difference between the lieutenant and me," he said to Ferrick. "He has to get permission from a judge to kick in your teeth. Not me."

Jericho told me he felt as if he was playing in some movie, some wild piece of camp. The villain was so perfectly cast, and he sounded to himself so pompously heroic. Underneath all that was a sickening anxiety for Pat Barry. He remembered his own words to Pascal the night before: *"Ferrick could use Pat to turn me helpless."* Exactly that had happened, and Ferrick's wry smile indicated that he knew that Jericho knew it. The next move would be dictated by Ferrick and his army of long-haired friends.

146

The moment of tension was broken by the sound of loud voices coming toward the toy-filled room from the other house. Perry charged in, followed by Al Stover and the two P.R. men. Perry was literally shaking himself loose from attempts to hold him back.

"Which of you is the cop in charge?" Perry demanded, looking from Meehan to Pascal.

"I'm Lieutenant Pascal."

"You came at just the right time, Lieutenant, which I suspect is a rarity for the police. I'm Perry Lewis. Someone in this house is trying to murder me. I need protection."

Pascal didn't look very interested.

"Ask him!" Perry shouted, pointing at Jericho.

Jericho answered Pascal's questioning glance with a brief outline of the story of the thermos jug. Ferrick listened, smiling and smiling.

"More guessarama," Pascal said grimly.

"You can't just brush it off," Perry said, "because there isn't any physical evidence left. I can tell you the most likely ones to have tried it. I can give you some pretty interesting dossiers on a half a dozen people, including my wife and her fancy Don Juan."

"You want to bring charges, you can come along with me to headquarters and make a formal statement," Pascal said.

"I'm not leaving here!" Perry said. "I'm not giving them a chance to plan it again."

"Please, Perry," Zelda said unsteadily. "You know you're

just inventing." She reached out to him, and he backed away as if her touch might be deadly.

"It's laughable!" he said hysterically. "Ferrick here is supposed to protect me, and he's the most likely one to have tried to do away with me!"

"Next week, *East Lynn,*" Ferrick said.

Al Stover tried to take charge. "I wonder if I could talk to you privately, Inspector," he said.

"Lieutenant," Pascal said.

At that point one of the other plain-clothes men joined them. "The two clowns back in there seem to be clean," he said. "They couldn't have been at your place, Lieutenant."

Pascal nodded slowly. He recognized a dead end when he saw one. He wasn't going to be able to place anyone here as having been a member of the party which had raided his apartment and taken Pat away. Not here and now, at any rate.

Al Stover forced a smile. "It's a little difficult to walk into this place cold, Lieutenant, and understand what makes the people here tick. It must sound a little wild to you, but really it's not so serious as it sounds. I know it must seem on the flamboyant side, but—"

"Flamboyant!" Pascal's voice was harsh. "Twenty-four hours ago someone tried to kill Jericho with a bomb. Tonight someone blew the lock off the door of my apartment, knocked me out, and kidnaped a girl. Yes, I'd call it flamboyant."

"But can you link any of the people here with those events, Lieutenant?"

148

"I didn't come here by accident," Pascal said.

"The wrong publicity, without proof, can be very costly to some very important people," Al said.

"Don't threaten the man, Stover," Jericho said.

Al shrugged. "If he makes a mistake, the repercussions in his department could be pretty earth-shaking."

"Thanks for being concerned for me," Pascal said dryly. He turned to Jericho. "Is there some place in this mad house where we could talk privately for a moment?"

"Privacy may be hard to come by," Jericho said. "Bugs, tape recorders, and hidden microphones are Perry's hobby."

"I couldn't care less," Pascal said. "I'd just like to talk to you without having to look at people who make my flesh creep." He turned and walked out of the room as though he meant it.

# Two

The place where Jericho and Pascal finally held a council of war was in a police car pulled up at the curb outside the Hell Hole. The party inside was growing. Taxis seemed to arrive in a steady stream, and there were half a dozen or more young men wearing the fancy-Dan trademark of Don Ferrick's jet-age Regency bucks.

Pascal watched a couple of them go in, frowning. "I can't get it out of my head that they aren't on the way to a costume ball," he said. "You know that Cardin, the French designer, is selling over six million dollars' worth of ready-made clothes a year in those Edwardian and Regency styles? He's just one." He shook his head. "Back in the twenties we thought the John Held flappers, with their open coats and flapping galoshes, were wild!"

Jericho was staring up at the three brownstones.

"What do we do about Pat?" he asked.

150

"There's a general alarm out," Pascal said. He didn't sound optimistic. "What would they look like if we cut their hair and put them in ordinary clothes?"

"Like the wildly discontented, disoriented, undisciplined anarchists they are," Jericho said. "What's frightening about them is a state of mind, not what they wear. They have nothing but contempt for squares like you and me who still live by some sort of code and believe in some sort of law and order. The birth-control pill has made sex a part of every date. They run in packs, and they're laughing at us right now because we're not up against one madman but a whole army of them. You thought Pat would be safe at your place because it never entered your head anyone would try to break into a policeman's home. We should have known she'd have to be surrounded by fifty patrolmen. God knows what she's facing at this moment."

"No one's molested you since last night," Pascal said. "You're the one who made Ferrick look like a clown."

"My time will come," Jericho said quietly. "There will presently be a message for me, asking me to go somewhere—with Pat as bait."

"So you don't go. Not alone," Pascal said.

"What else?" Jericho said. "They just might let her go in exchange for me. I'll have to take that chance if that's how they play it." He drew a deep breath. "Zelda's chauffeur told me there's some kind of club on the upper East Side where these fancy boys hole up. It's the only lead I've got, Dave. Could you justify a raid on that joint? Your people must know about it. You were gone over by some fancy boys. This club is a hangout for them."

Pascal reached forward and switched on the car's two-way radio. He requested information.

"It's called the Brighton Club," a metallic voice answered. "I'll dig out the address for you, Lieutenant. We've been praying for some kind of excuse to unload on 'em, but so far they're clean. The precinct captain up there—Brodsky—may have a file on the place. I'll get him to call you back."

"I'll stay put here in Car Thirty-seven," Pascal said.

Static took over.

"About your murder theory," Pascal said, leaning back in the seat. His eyes were tired. Jericho guessed he had a splitting headache. Square fingers touched the adhesive patch over the right temple.

"It's pure theory from your point of view," Jericho said.

"Perry Lewis seems to buy it."

"I'll make you a bet," Jericho said. "If you could make a rigid check on the twenty-five people closest to Perry, you'd find that twenty-four of them use sleeping pills or pep pills. Twenty-four of 'em would have access to what killed Tommy Nolan—and to that thermos jug."

"But all twenty-four of them wouldn't feel murderous about him."

"I wonder," Jericho said. "Zelda is the queen bee of that hive. Zelda is the one they love, the high priestess of a sort of youth cult. Perry can only get the kind of attention he must have by using his power over her, hurting her and everyone else who comes in range."

152

"So she fights."

"Zelda likes to be hurt," Jericho said, his face hard. "Perry is her bed of nails, the hot coals she walks on. The techniques of masochism were invented for her."

The radio sputtered. "Calling Car Thirty-seven.'

Pascal threw the switch and identified himself.

"Captain Brodsky here, Lieutenant. You were making inquiries about the Brighton Club?"

"Yes."

"Figure it might have something to do with the raid on your apartment?"

"Yes."

"Could be," Brodsky said. He sounded doubtful. "You know anything about the club?"

"No."

"It might surprise you."

"After tonight I can't be surprised," Pascal said.

"We've had our eye on it for some time," Brodsky said. "Thought it might be a headquarters for some sort of orgies. We thought they might be selling liquor illegally and we got a warrant to have a look around."

"And?"

"No violations," Brodsky said. "The members have lockers and keep their own supply of liquors. The club provides ice, glasses, and setups. All meticulously within the law. The place is an eyeful."

"In what way?"

"It's like a museum. Oriental rugs. Magnificent furniture out of the Regency period. Portraits that belong in a gallery. Silverware and china you wouldn't believe. Glass chandeliers. The whole thing is elegance in spades, Lieutenant. It's spotlessly kept. Nobody lives there except a couple—house servants—but there are half a dozen bedrooms, furnished in the same richness, where friends from out of town can spend a night or two." Brodsky began to sound poetic. "It's a place where you come in from the hot sun and noise of the city into coolness and quietness and perfection of taste. Somebody has spent a hell of a lot of money there."

"No complaints from the neighbors?"

"None."

"Why were you interested?"

"The long-haired creeps that come and go," Brodsky said. "Cuckie clothes. You know?"

"I know. How do I get in?" Pascal asked.

"Guest card."

"Don't be an idiot," Pascal said sharply. "How does a policeman get in—without a warrant?"

Brodsky was silent for a moment. "After what happened to you tonight? We have a file on the club. There are some newspaper clippings. Someone—maybe Norton Mockridge—did a piece on it. There's a photograph of the secretary—guy named Joel Evergreen."

"You're kidding!"

"His father is Charles Evergreen, president of God knows how many companies and chairman of God knows how many boards of directors. Triplex apartment on Park Avenue, summer place at Southampton, winter place at

154

Camden, villa in the south of France."

"Interesting, but how does that get me in? I don't rub elbows with Charles Evergreen."

"You looked at our file, looking for longhairs. You thought you recognized Joel Evergreen as one of the people who broke into your place. It's enough. You want a couple of boys from here to go with you?"

"I'll stop by your precinct house in ten minutes," Pascal said.

"It's a waste of time," Jericho said, when the car radio was switched off. "It's obviously their legitimate front. House servants. They won't be holding an unwilling prisoner there."

"I have to start somewhere," Pascal said.

"I have a feeling I should light by a phone," Jericho said. He looked up at the brownstones. "They're not going to get any message to me, sitting beside you in a police car."

"I suppose I know better than to argue with you," Pascal said. "Nobody's going to gain by your lying down on the railroad tracks and waiting for the midnight express to do you in."

"If it wasn't for Pat! I got her into this."

"If I remember right, she got you into it," Pascal said. He touched the bump on his head and winced. "If you're sure you're going to be invited into a meat chopper, I'd stay away from phones and invitations of any sort. The odds aren't good any way you play it, but if I were in your shoes, I think I'd go back inside and ask Don boy to lay it

155

on the line. The place is lousy with witnesses. All we need, Johnny, is one slip from Ferrick and we can move in. We can't rubber-hose him at the nearest precinct house, but if you can goad him into one small indiscretion—"

Jericho looked as though he was coming back to life again.

"You join me?" he asked.

"Nothing will happen with me there, or my boys, beyond a request to stop you from throwing your weight around," Pascal said. "I'll leave a patrol car circling the block in case you yell for help."

"And you?"

"Maybe Mr. Joel Evergreen will point his aristocratic nose in an interesting direction if I apply a little pressure," Pascal said.

Jericho massaged his right fist in the palm of his left hand. "If I get the word to go somewhere for Pat, that will be that," he said.

Pascal's smile was grim. "You could try leaving a trail of peanut shells for me to follow," he said. . . .

Pascal went back into the house to call off his men. As the front door was opened for the lieutenant by Eddie, the sounds of laughter and music welled out onto the street for a moment and then were cut off by the closed door.

Jericho got out of the police car. His muscles felt stiff, and he had the impulse to stretch. It was a familiar feeling, one that often came over him when he was faced with some sort of physical action.

It was just a few minutes past two in the morning. Jericho glanced down the block. A girl in slacks and wearing a leather jacket was walking two miniature poodles. There were only a few lights in windows of the other houses. The rain of the morning before had been blown away, and the sky was dotted with stars, pale behind the general illumination from the city. There were hundreds of people within shouting distance, Jericho thought, who had gone to bed in what must seem to them an ordinary, routine world. Later on this new day some of them would go to church; some would just stay at home and read the Sunday papers, watch television, or putter around with some hobby. They would read about violence in the papers, but they were convinced that sort of thing didn't happen to people you knew. If they'd happened to look out the window and seen the police car outside Zelda's three brownstones, they'd have thought, "Another wild party," and gone back to bed. Murder and kidnaping would have been the farthest thoughts from their minds. And, Jericho thought bitterly, if he were suddenly to shout for help, not a single one of them would respond. He'd be lucky if someone got up nerve enough to call the police.

Pascal came back out of the house with the other detectives. They stood in a small huddle around Jericho.

"Meehan will patrol the block in case you need him," Pascal said. "I've told him that if you don't show in, say, an hour and a half, he's to go in looking for you."

Jericho was staring at the front door of the Hell Hole.

"What happens in there will be kid stuff," he said. He looked at Pascal. "If I come out and head someplace, Meehan isn't to follow me. That will certainly be one of the conditions they make."

"You can at least give him some sort of high sign," Pascal said, "which will tell him you've had the word."

"If I give him any sort of sign or stop to speak to him, it'll mean I haven't had a message. No sign will be the sign."

Pascal nodded. "I'm not behaving like a policeman," he said. "I shouldn't be letting you do this."

"We don't have much choice, do we, Dave?"

"Bastards!" Pascal said, scowling at the house.

"See you around," Jericho said. He drew a deep breath and walked up the steps to the front door. He heard the police car start away from the curb behind him.

Eddie answered Jericho's ring. His chauffeur's jacket had been replaced by a white houseman's coat. He looked surprised.

"You back," he said.

"Me back," Jericho said, and walked into the little entrance hall.

The noise from upstairs was loud and raucous. A set of drums, a bass, and a clarinet had joined Jimmy Cooper's piano in the music department. Feet bounded on the floor in a rhythmic beat. Voices were shrill, the laughter sounding forced.

"Stirrup cup?" Eddie suggested, moving toward the little service bar.

"Thanks, no," Jericho said. He hunched his broad shoul-

158

ders under his brown tweed jacket.

"The boss is out of his cotton-picking mind," Eddie said. "Drunk as a coot and brandishing a machine pistol at any one who comes near him. Won't let anyone mix a drink for him. You try to scare him to death, or is there anything to the idea the stuff that killed Nolan was meant for him?"

"You pays your money and you takes your choice," Jericho said. "I think there's plenty to it."

"You watch the crowd come in?" Eddie asked. "There's maybe a dozen of Ferrick's Regency boys up there now. You should be nice and quiet and polite, I think."

"And if I'm not?"

"Well, the two of us won't get very far against that mob, but we can give it the old college try," Eddie said.

"You're on my team?"

Eddie grinned. "Let's say I'm not on Don boy's team," he said.

Jericho walked slowly up the stairs to the second floor. Bacchanalia, he thought. Almost everyone was involved in a wild kind of dance, flushed with excitement. Three of the Regency boys had joined Jimmy Cooper in the making of the music. They were a better-than-good combo. An entirely strange girl spun out of the dancing throng, threw her arms around Jericho's neck, gave him a very hard kiss on the mouth, and whirled away, screaming with laughter.

Jericho looked over the tops of heads, trying to spot the principals in the act.

At the far end of the room Perry sat cross-legged on his

159

divan. His eyes, even at this distance, were bright, hot, angry. The famous thermos jug was in his left hand, and as Eddie had said, a machine pistol lay in his lap. Jericho saw there was a silencer fixed to the band. A few steps away Don Ferrick was in a huddle with three of the Regency boys. At the bar Rich Ragsdale was involved in an uncharacteristically animated conversation with a pale-faced Zelda. Al Stover and the P.R. boys were evidently in a huddle somewhere else. The dark, ivory-skinned Lillian Heller was alone at the far end of the bar. She looked frightened. She seemed to be the first one aware of Jericho's return.

Jericho edged his way around the dance floor, passing close to the music.

"Welcome, man!" Jimmy Cooper shouted at him, cigar bobbing between uneven, stained teeth.

The clarinet player blew three very sharp, discordant notes on his black stick. It was clearly meant to attract Ferrick's attention. He and his three friends were suddenly focusing on Jericho. Jericho's smile was amiable as he waved at them. His course was charted to bring him up alongside Lillian Heller, who was gripping the bar as though she needed it for support.

"For someone who doesn't enjoy taking off her clothes in public, you spend a lot of time in this place, ma'am," he said. He stood beside her, his back to the wall. He remembered Eddie's advice about his "rearview mirror." "Where's Al?"

"Nick Glass is here," she said unsteadily. "They're

somewhere, trying to decide what to do about the special. They have to go before the cameras Monday morning or be in overtime troubles with the unions."

"A few little things like murder and kidnaping shouldn't bother them," Jericho said. "I should think they might even hypo the Neilson ratings."

"Al believes that if Zelda and Rich Ragsdale are in the clear they should be able to go ahead," Lillian said.

"Has anyone suggested they aren't?"

"I don't know. You're the one, Mr. Jericho, who's making all the trouble."

"And I'm not in the special," Jericho said, "so they should feel as happy as can be." He moved around behind the bar. The party seemed to be on a help-yourself basis.

"Can't you drop your own fight until it's over?" Lillian asked.

"Hasn't anyone told you what happened tonight?" Jericho asked. "Hasn't anyone told you about Pat Barry?"

"What about her?"

"Get Al to tell you," Jericho said. He poured some whiskey into a tall glass with ice. Then he looked around the back bar and located a bottle of grenadine. He filled the glass with it, producing a bright scarlet drink. Lillian stared at it.

"You drink that sticky mess?" she asked.

"I'm an artist. I like color," he said, but he didn't drink. "You're a nice girl, Lillian," he said. "You love your guy. You stand by him in trouble. Take advice. Get out of here and take him with you. You don't belong in this world.

161

Buy a little gas station in the country and settle down to living and loving."

He gave her a broad smile and moved away, glass in hand. He proceeded, almost languidly, to the place where Ferrick and the three Regency boys stood watching his approach.

"Nice party," Jericho said.

The four long-haired young men in their fancy frock coats stared at him. They looked, he thought, like something out of an ancient horror movie.

"I thought you might have had sense enough not to come back here," Ferrick said.

"I had a reason," Jericho said. "I don't like your necktie and I didn't have a chance to tell you before." Very deliberately he threw the red, sticky contents of his glass at Ferrick's frilly shirt front and all over the flowered cravat. Behind him he heard Lillian Heller scream, and the music stopped in mid beat.

Ferrick's face was marble-white as he instinctively dabbed at his shirt front with a handkerchief. One of the Regency boys swung at Jericho. Jericho took a quick side step and brought a sharp uppercut to the young man's jaw. He went down to his knees, a little trickle of blood erupting from the corner of his mouth. Jericho dropped his glass, and it smashed on the hardwood floor. He was smiling at Ferrick, inviting him to act.

No one else moved. They were waiting for some sort of sign from Ferrick. The other Regency boys on the dance floor had moved in quickly to make a circle around

Jericho.

"Everyone knows that it's no trick for a dozen strong young men to wipe up the floor with one strong old guy like me," Jericho said. "It would hardly prove that you're up to handling a situation like this without help, Don boy. It's my humble opinion you haven't the guts to go it alone."

Ferrick's eyes were blazing.

"I've heard a lot about what a tough crew you have," Jericho went on in a conversational tone, "but I question your personal courage. I don't think you've got what it takes."

There was a throaty growl from the battalion of Regency boys.

"I expect to be summoned to the slaughter at any minute," Jericho said, "but it would give me great satisfaction to prove, publicly, that you're a cringing coward."

"And you'll get the chance, John boy!" Perry Lewis shouted from behind them. He was standing up on his divan, dancing up and down like a child on a box spring. He was aiming his machine pistol, silencer hanging on its barrel, in the general direction of the circle of Regency boys around Jericho. "First one who interferes gets a slug in the back of the head!"

At the moment Zelda swept into the center of the circle. She stood between Jericho and Ferrick. "Please!" she cried out. "Oh, please, please!"

Out of the corner of his eye Jericho saw Ragsdale at the divan, talking urgently but softly to Perry. And through

163

the door leading to the next house came Al Stover, Nick Glass, and the two P.R. men.

Zelda had turned to Ferrick. Her arms were around him, and she was whispering urgently to him. The quiet was broken; everyone started to talk and laugh with an overriding hysteria.

The men from TAB had also surrounded Perry.

Jericho's eyes never left Ferrick's face. He saw Zelda step away from Ferrick and the front of her simple yellow dress was stained with the red syrup of Jericho's thrown drink.

Al Stover joined Jericho. "Are you out of your mind?" he demanded. "Isn't there any way you can be persuaded not to muck up our lives and our business? I came out here to find you and I walk into this."

"What did you want to find me for?" Jericho asked, not taking his eyes off Ferrick.

"There's a phone call for you," Al said.

For the first time Ferrick's face broke out of its rock-hard mask. One corner of his mouth moved down in a mocking smile.

Jericho felt his stomach muscles tighten. "Saved by the bell," he said to Ferrick. He turned away to Al. "Where's the phone?"

"First door to your right as you start down the hall. And for God's sake, Jericho, take it easy!"

"It seems I'm not being given a choice," Jericho said.

He turned his back on the frock-coated circle, walked directly between two of the long-haired gentry, and made

164

for the door at the corner of the room.

The music started again in a blare of sound.

The first door to the right down the corridor opened into what was evidently used as an office. On the desk was a telephone, its receiver lying on a blotting pad. Jericho stared at it for a second and then he picked it up.

"Jericho here," he said.

"I take it you are interested in the safe return of Miss Barry," a voice said. It sounded as Pat Barry had described it, cultivated, meticulous, as though it might be faked.

"Very interested," Jericho said.

"We can negotiate," the voice said.

"When and where?"

"Take the Lexington Avenue subway—local train—downtown," the voice said. "At one of the local stops someone will contact you. If you're not alone, you will have taken the trip in vain."

"I'll be alone," Jericho said.

"Then start now," the voice said.

There was a click as the phone was hung up at the other end—and then the dial tone. Jericho put the receiver back in its cradle. He was being asked to walk into an unbreakable trap. His impulse was to go back into the other room and smash the truth out of Ferrick, but from somewhere the sound of Pat's voice echoed in his ears, saying, *"Johnny, I want that year! I want it!"* He'd gotten her into this. He had to get her out, regardless of the risk.

He walked slowly back along the corridor to the party

room. Ferrick was gone, and so were the three Regency boys who'd been close to him. Zelda appeared to have gone with them. Jericho walked quickly around the edge of the dance floor and down the stairs to the entrance hall. Eddie was there, his face split in a broad grin.

"You made him back away!" he said. "Boy, it was worth the price of admission."

"He leave?" Jericho asked.

"Not this way," Eddie said. "I imagine he went into the next house to wipe the gook off his front or maybe get himself a clean outfit. He has a wardrobe over there in Zelda's quarters. Where you headed?"

"Fresh air," Jericho said grimly.

The street outside was deserted. The air was cool and fresh. Jericho started west toward Lexington Avenue. Before he reached the corner, the police car with Meehan and his partner in it came cruising along. Jericho didn't even look at them. No sign was the sign that he'd heard. There was nothing Pascal or Meehan or anyone could do if he was to give Pat the chance for freedom. Clean up afterward, he thought. That was all they could do.

Jericho had faced a great many dangerous situations in his life. He told me afterward that as he walked along the almost deserted streets he felt a fatalistic sense of doom for the first time in his experience. He had always been prepared to fight back in tough spots. This time he was to be a sacrificial lamb. He remembered Al Stover's earlier warning: *"Ferrick is a crippler. I know one guy who hasn't been out of a wheel chair since he crossed Ferrick."*

166

Jericho had seen the truth of that in Ferrick's amber-cold eyes.

As he approached the subway entrance outside the darkened windows of Bloomingdale's, every instinct told him to turn back. How would they "negotiate"? Unless they had Pat with them and turned her free before him, there'd be no way of knowing that there really were any negotiations. He was playing a hundred-to-one shot. All they really wanted was to get him in some isolated spot and give him the full dose of Ferrick medicine. It wouldn't help Pat. He could almost feel the pain of an inescapable beating and torture.

He stood at the head of the dark stairway leading down onto the station platform. The palms of his huge hands were damp with sweat. Then, slowly, he started down.

He stopped at the change booth to buy a couple of subway tokens. The man in the booth was reading an early-morning copy of the *News*. He didn't even look up at his customer. Jericho could have sworn he hadn't been followed, but he knew some of the Regency boys could have been planted along the way and passed the word of his coming. There seemed to be no one else on the semidark platform, but each dark shadow produced a suggestion of menace.

It seemed forever and was perhaps twenty minutes before he heard the distant rumble of an approaching train. They run infrequently at that hour of the morning. Jericho's muscles tensed. He was now the hunted animal. He half expected some sort of wild rush out of the darkness that would catapult him down under the grinding wheels of the train.

There was nothing. He was the only traveler to board the train as its doors slid automatically open.

There were only five or six people in the car, including three elderly women who must be going to or returning from nighttime cleaning jobs. An unshaven drunk was sprawled on the seat opposite Jericho. Two men in work clothes sat separate from each other at the far end of the car, reading newspapers. An indifferent trainman looked through the dirty glass partition in the door at the other end.

As the train slowed for the stop at Grand Central, Jericho felt himself tensing. At one of the local stops he was to be contacted. But there was no sign of interest in him from the eight or ten new passengers who came into the car.

The train started again. As it pulled into the next stop, a large woman wearing a black shawl over her head brushed against Jericho.

"Twenty-third Street is your stop, Jericho," a husky voice said.

Jericho spun around, but the door was already closing on the shawled woman who had stepped out onto the platform. As she hurried away, Jericho could have sworn no woman could have managed the long, half-running strides.

Jericho moved out onto the back platform of the train. As he stood there, swaying slightly in the rocking movement of the car, he noticed a length of chain hanging from a metal hook. It was used to block off the rear end of the car if it happened to be the last one on the train. Jericho took it quickly off the hook and stuffed it into the pocket of his coat, his right hand closed around it. It would help him to do a little damage when the climax moment arrived.

The train speed slackened as they came into the station. It stopped. The doors opened with a hiss of air. Jericho stepped out.

Two or three other passengers got off the train further up the platform. They headed for the exits leading up to the street. The train doors closed, and it pulled away into the dark tunnel beyond.

The platform was deserted. Jericho moved away from the front edge and crossed to stand with his back to the inner wall. He took the chain out of his pocket and held it, doubled, hanging at his side.

And then he saw them.

They came out of both exits at either end of the platform. They came out of the men's toilet and the women's toilet. Two of them went to the change booth, and a startled old man was pulled out of the booth and held between them. They were dressed for *le sport*; turtle-necked sweaters, corduroy pants in blue and red and yellow. Some of them wore absurd little caps perched on top of their long, thick hairdos. They came toward Jericho from both sides, unhurried. There was plenty of time. It would be twenty minutes before another train came. Cold bastards, Jericho thought. And then he shouted at them.

"Who does the negotiating?" His voice echoed and re-echoed in the cavernous station.

Somebody laughed, and they edged forward, languid, unhurried. Jericho knew there would be a sudden concerted rush. He took a step away from the wall to give himself more room to swing the chain. He noticed that most of them were wearing sandals which made a queer shuffling sound as they moved in toward him.

"I think you'd better listen to me," Jericho said, loud and clear. "I came here in good faith to negotiate for the release of the girl. Somebody better talk, or they'll be taking more than just me away from here in the morgue basket." He swung the chain, gently, like a pendulum. Their faces were more than a blur now. Cold faces. They looked like young men who rarely, if ever, smiled.

Jericho swung the chain, its arc a little wider. "Maybe you better draw lots for who comes in first," he said. "I warn you that the first two or three of you aren't going anywhere afterward. I came here to make a deal, but if this is the way you want it . . ."

They seemed to stop, sullen, staring. They looked absurd, like mannequins in a shopwindow. Dislocated children, Jericho thought, but dangerous.

From some distance away came the sound of a strange, eerie whistle. Heads half turned. For a fraction of time Jericho shared their attention with that long, thin whistle. It seemed to leave them uncertain.

Then, on a signal that Jericho missed, they came at him,

170

an explosive human tidal wave. Only a trained fighter could have done anything but fall under that first charge. Jericho didn't go down. The chain swung savagely, like a whip, and the voice of the crowd rose in an angry roar. He saw someone go down with a red gash at eye level. They were at the narrow portion of the platform, near the tunnel mouth, and that flailing chain kept his attackers from getting behind Jericho. The first line of Regency boys took a bad beating for seconds, and then the sheer weight of numbers proved to be too much. Someone caught the chain and hung onto it for dear life so that Jericho couldn't swing it. He dropped it and concentrated on the man directly in front of him. His left hand fastened in the long wavy hair, and he yanked the startled face close enough to smash his right fist full into a mouth that had opened to scream.

That was all he remembered. Something exploded inside his head and he went down, vaguely aware of pounding fists and fingernails that tore at his flesh like fishhooks.

# Three

I had spent most of that night sitting near the telephone in the living room of my apartment, waiting for a call from Jericho that never came. I couldn't concentrate on work, or even on the Kennedy book I'd been reading a couple of days before. It was about three in the morning when I dozed off in my armchair. No news, I told myself, was good news. I cursed Jericho mildly for not keeping me posted.

The phone woke me. It was daylight. The city was quiet—Sunday-morning quiet.

Pascal's voice was unnaturally casual.

"Jericho bring any fresh clothes to your place, Hallam?"

"Yes."

"Bring him a complete change except for shoes," Pascal said.

"Bring them where?" I said.

"Medical East," he said.

"What's he doing in a hospital?" I asked.

"Long story," Pascal said. "But hurry. He's not an easy patient."

It seems that almost as Jericho felt consciousness slipping away under the shower of blows from the Regency boys, there was an interruption that saved his life. Half a dozen cops with drawn guns had appeared on the subway platform. That whistle Jericho had heard had evidently been the warning of approaching trouble from a lookout for the Regency boys. The longhairs were running for safety as the cops appeared. Some shots were fired in the air. Two of the flying mob were grabbed by the cops, and there were three more lying unconscious beside Jericho on the platform.

Jericho was muttering Pascal's name as they knelt beside him.

The arrival of the cops was not a fluke. They'd received an anonymous phone call at the local precinct house telling them that there was a rumble coming up at the Twenty-third Street subway station. A big red-bearded man was about to be taken over by a gang of longhairs. They'd made it, not quite in time, but soon enough to save Jericho from what might have been a fatal beating.

Who had made the phone call? That was an answer no one had when I arrived at Medical East. I got a quick rundown on the night's madness from Pascal as he met me in the lobby and took me up to the tenth floor where Jericho was in a private room.

173

Jericho's mutterings on the subway platform had prompted the local man in charge to contact the Homicide man. The result was that Jericho was taken to Medical East instead of Bellevue and promptly attended by Pascal's own doctor.

"X-rays are negative," Pascal told me, "but he took a bad beating and may have a concussion. The doctor wants him to stay here for a day, but I think we'll have to strap him down to make it stick."

That was when I got my first sketchy account of what the evening had contained in the way of action. And I'd been dozing over a book!

Jericho looked as if he'd been hit by a truck. He was lying back against the pillows on his slightly raised hospital bed.

"Well, I see you didn't need any help," I said.

"I got help," he said. "The interesting question is, where did I get it from?"

"The anonymous caller had to know exactly where the rumble was planned," Pascal said.

"I thought of Zelda herself," Jericho said. "She might have thought her boy friend would get into too much trouble. But they tell me the caller was a man."

"Perry?" I suggested. "He's not a Ferrick lover and might have enjoyed fouling up Don boy's plans."

"There's no time for guessing games," Jericho said. He sat up and his face twisted in a sudden spasm of pain. "They never meant to negotiate for Pat. They just meant to get me to that station platform and let me have it. It's clear we're not going to help Pat by playing the game their way."

"So we do nothing for her?" I asked.

"There's a city-wide alarm out for her," Pascal said. "Every hangout for Ferrick's kind of boy is being watched. We're questioning and checking. We have five boys who were involved in the attack on Johnny. Three of them aren't in very good shape, but the other two—"

"Where the hell are my clothes?" Jericho shouted. He sounded almost normal. . . .

My contact so far with the Regency boys had been very slight. I'd seen Ferrick and a couple of his friends for the short time at Zelda's when Jericho was draping Ferrick over the chair there. They looked like freaks. I thought of them as freaks. I was totally unprepared for the two young men we encountered at the precinct house about a half an hour later, after Jericho had talked his way out of Medical East over the doctor's protests and hand-washings. Perhaps I should have been forewarned by Pascal's account of what he'd discovered at the Brighton Club. Brodsky, the precinct captain, hadn't exaggerated.

"It is one of the most unexpected places," Pascal said. "Expensively put together, tasteful. A library that would make your eyes pop. An elaborate stereo system and a collection of modern recordings that probably can't be duplicated anywhere. In its way it out-swanks any rich man's club I've ever been in. My questions were answered by an impeccable young gentleman in a green frock coat, hair permanently waved down over his ears, who turned out to be Mr. Joel Evergreen. He looked at me as if I were a candidate for the state mental hospital when I suggested I'd like to look around for a girl prisoner. I was taken from cellar to rooftop by a white-coated houseman who opened any doors I asked him to open. I was eventually offered a very dry martini with a spot of imported caviar on a slice of crisp melba toast." Pascal sighed. "This place is an exclusive, perfectly run gentlemen's club. It's as clean as the antimacassars on your grandmother's living-room chairs."

"And Ferrick is a member?" Jericho asked.

"He is, no less, chairman of the Board of Trustees."

The two young men who'd been grabbed on the subway platform were brought to us in the office of the precinct captain. Somehow I thought of them as kids, but these were mature, hard, contemptuous men in their late twenties. Pascal glanced over some papers the precinct captain handed him. He looked up, his face unreadable.

"You are Herman Melville?" he asked the first young man, who stood, relaxed, in his blue turtle-neck sweater and yellow corduroys.

"I am," he said.

"And you," Pascal said to the other one, "are Charles Dickens?"

"I am," the second one said. His colors were red and green.

"Oh, come on!" Jericho said from the corner of the bare office.

"Driver's licenses and other documents verify," Pascal

said. "The names were not assumed for this particular moment, at least." He put the papers down on the desk. "You have been held for questioning pending formal charges."

The one who called himself Melville smiled a thin, hard smile. "There's no mystery about anything," he said.

"You were part of a gang which attacked Mr. Jericho on the Twenty-third Street platform of the East Side I.R.T.?"

"I was," Melville said.

"We were," Charles Dickens said.

"It was a planned rumble?" Pascal asked.

"'Rumble' is street-urchin jargon," Herman Melville said. "Mr. Jericho, as I understand it, was invited to be present. He came."

"And some twenty of you attacked him," Pascal said.

"I won't split hairs with you," Melville said. "Only two or three of us could get at him at one time. There were actually eighteen of us there on the platform."

"Waiting for him to arrive?"

"Well, we waited on the stairways and in the rest rooms until he appeared. Incidentally, the condition of the rest rooms is unspeakable!"

"I'll make a note," Pascal said. "What was the purpose of this convention of creeps?"

The Charles Dickens one made an impatient gesture. "If you want to ask us questions, Lieutenant, we'll try to answer them. If this is just an occasion for cheap insults—"

"My apologies," Pascal said, with a grave little bow. "Could I persuade you to tell me just what it was all about?"

"There are a great many people in this world who live both inside and outside the law. Your friend Jericho is one of them."

"Could you elaborate?" Pascal asked, a gentle mockery hiding what I knew must be a massive effort at self-control.

"It's simple enough," Herman Melville said. "Jericho can walk, uninvited, into a party, steal a painting, and knock a man unconscious with a dangerous karate blow that might well have been fatal. He can make a comic spectacle of his victim. And he can walk out under the full protection of the so-called law. No one will lift a finger to stop him. That's what Charles meant by both inside and outside the law. We are very familiar with the fact that the antiquated hero symbols of our society, like Jericho, are immune from punishment when they break the law. We let our hair grow long and a bartender may be arrested for serving us drinks on the ground that we are homosexuals. We are symbols of decay, in your eyes, and we can't cross the street without walking into trouble. Does the law say we must crew-cut our hair? Does the law say we must conform to Madison Avenue tailoring? No, but because we don't conform, we are given a double dose of the self-righteous pomposity that rules your society. We know that the law will never punish Jericho for his behavior, so"—he shrugged—"we took his punishment into our own hands."

"Beginning with the bombing of his apartment?"

"The only questions we can answer," Charles Dickens said, "are ones we know the answers to as a result of personal involvement. We don't know about the bombing."

"You know about it, but you mean you weren't there."

"We weren't there," Melville said.

"Were you at my apartment last night when someone blew the lock off the door and kidnaped a guest of mine?" Pascal asked.

"We weren't there," Melville said.

Jericho was suddenly out of the corner, towering in front of the two Regency boys. "Where are you holding Patricia Barry?" he demanded.

The one called Melville eyed him steadily. "I suppose the law will turn its back while you try to beat information out of us we don't have," he said. "You see what I mean? The law is a convenience tool for your kind. It's a hostile weapon against our kind. It will find some way to excuse your taking a violent action against us, but it will be solemnly outraged at the notion that we took a violent action against you."

"Lay off, Johnny," Pascal said in a tired voice.

It was pretty obvious we weren't going to get anywhere with Herman Melville and Charles Dickens. In their own rebellious world they were living up to the concept of name, rank, and serial number.

"You want to make a formal charge against these two, Johnny?" Pascal asked.

"No," Jericho said, not taking his bright, cold eyes off the two Regency boys. "Turn 'em loose. I want them to carry the news. Let your friends know that I'm beginning to think of the law as an encumbrance too." His voice lowered so that Pascal and I could barely hear him. "I want Patricia Barry back. Each hour I have to wait makes me less reasonable. You're forcing me to live in your jungle, friends. You may be surprised how efficiently I can adjust to it." He turned and walked over to the far corner of the room. The two Regency boys watched him, smiling smugly.

Pascal signaled to the uniformed cop by the door to take the two longhairs back to the detention room. The minute the door closed on them Jericho spun around.

"They have a genius for it! They make you do it!" he said angrily.

"Do what?" Pascal asked.

"Sound like a pompous hero out of a Jane Austen novel. Did you hear me, bellowing threats up the rainspout! The truth is I can't adjust efficiently to their world. I don't understand them. I don't know how. I can run around in circles knocking heads together, and what'll it get me? A mass violence I can't handle."

Pascal had walked around behind the precinct captain's roll-top desk. He had taken a pipe out of his pocket and was filling it slowly.

"Should we call it the square response to the round approach?" he asked dryly. "I listened to you, Johnny, and I felt for you. I know how desperately you'd like to get Ferrick in a corner and beat the truth out of him. It would be wonderfully satisfying. I'd enjoy getting in a few licks of

180

my own. But you're right. They have a genius for making us act like the squares we are and then laughing themselves sick in private. It's not, however, a new experience for a cop—being laughed at by the anarchistic type of mind. You're not a good cop until you can swallow insults and ignore provocation. If the cop reacts the way you do and finally is driven to knocking a few heads together, the cry of 'police brutality' goes up all over the city."

"So where are we?" Jericho asked. I thought I'd never heard him sound so completely defeated. "We let them have their fun with Pat, God help her. We let them run over us like a stampeding herd. We swallow their insults and ignore their provocations and get nowhere. Where are we, Dave?"

Pascal held a lighter to the bowl of his pipe. "I listened to you telling them how thick the hair is on your chest, Johnny, and I got thinking," he said. "We've been so busy he-manning it that we've overlooked our very best chance."

Jericho's head came up.

"You have a weapon, Johnny, you've forgotten."

"Weapon?"

"You have control of the use of Tommy Nolan's paintings. Twenty-four hours from now they start shooting the Zelda special at the Brooklyn studios of TAB. There's something like a million dollars involved, a solid hunk of it already irrevocably spent. Behind the operation is a great broadcasting empire and a powerful manufacturing company that sells its product all over the world. They control companies, corporations, stocks, bonds—money! This is a power complex that would make the United States Government hesitate about crossing it." Pascal smiled. "Suggest anything to you?"

I suddenly saw them sitting around the conference table at TAB: Nick Glass, the little Napoleon, Max Morrison, the lawyer with the Mount Rushmore face, the anxious Al Stover, the shrewd Maury Zimmerman, the yes men, the P.R. men with their pencils poised. Comic in a way, and yet, as Pascal said, they represented almost unthinkable power if they chose to concentrate it

"What are we waiting for?" Jericho asked, his voice suddenly buoyant.

# Four

The little Napoleon had had less than two hours' sleep when Jericho and I invaded his suite at the Waldorf. He had settled his problems at Zelda's place; he had made the decision to go on with the special and so arranged it that, if it was the wrong decision, Al Stover, Rich Ragsdale, and others would be the goats.

Al Stover, distracted sounding, had told us that we'd find Nick Glass at a suite Trans American kept permanently at the Waldorf. It was about seven-thirty on Sunday morning, an unheard-of time to call any executive of any company, let alone one connected even remotely with show business. Al, I gathered, would be flogging the horses as hard as he could to get to the Waldorf as quickly as we did.

Pascal was not with us. It wasn't quite ethical for a policeman to be present at what amounted to a little well-bred blackmailing.

Nick Glass, in a blue silk dressing gown, opened the door of his suite to us. He tried to look cheerful, but he wasn't too successful.

"Look, fellows," he said, "I've had a rough night. I can't imagine what could be so important, but you made it sound as if—"

He shrugged and led us into his sitting room. I could smell fresh coffee from somewhere and was grateful for the prospect.

"Say, what happened to you?" Nick asked when he got a good look at Jericho.

"Hit and run," Jericho said.

"Sorry to hear it. But look, fellows—"

"You heard a lot of wild talk tonight, didn't you, Mr. Glass?" Jericho said. "Somebody trying to murder Perry, for instance?"

"Show-business people always exaggerate," Nick said.

"You hope," Jericho said.

"Say, I wish I hadn't missed that drink-throwing episode," Nick said. "Never could go for Ferrick and his crowd. But Zelda insists—so I mean—"

"Did anyone tell you about the Regency boys who blew the lock off the front door of a detective's apartment and kidnaped the lady who has control of Tommy Nolan's paintings?"

"Horseplay of some sort," Nick muttered. "Coffee?"

"Thanks," I said.

Nick puttered around in a serving pantry and came

184

back with three cups of coffee on a tray. "Now," he said, "you said on the phone something important was cooking." His laugh was forced. "Somehow you convinced me, or you wouldn't be here at this ghastly hour."

"It's simple," Jericho said. "Horseplay or not, someone kidnaped Patricia Barry some hours ago."

Nick Glass clucked and shook his head.

"I want her back," Jericho said.

"Well, naturally. Lovely girl from all accounts," Nick said.

"Yeah. Lovely. Now here's how it is, Mr. Glass."

"Nick!" Glass protested. "Everybody calls me Nick."

"Okay, Nick. Here's how it is. It is now twenty minutes to eight. I want to meet Miss Barry in the Palm Court at the Plaza at exactly ten o'clock."

"Who wouldn't?" Nick said. He looked around for a yes man to laugh at his joke, but there was only Jericho and me, and we didn't laugh.

The doorbell rang and the little Napoleon looked relieved. He excused himself and immediately reappeared, followed by Al Stover, worn-looking and needing a shave.

"You're just in time for the ultimatum, Al," Jericho said.

"Couldn't whatever it is wait until we've had a little rest?" Al asked.

"It couldn't," Jericho said. "You and Nick here are going to have to go to work. You haven't remarked on my bruises, Al. I was thinking about you when I got them. Ferrick, you told me, is a crippler. You're right, old boy. I just got out of it by luck. Now—listen, because it seems

185

foolish to have to say it more than once. I want to meet Pat Barry in the Palm Court at the Plaza at ten o'clock this morning."

Al looked puzzled. "So—?"

"Make sure that she's there," Jericho said.

"Are you asking us to make a date for you?" Glass asked. "If this is some kind of a perverted joke—after last night—"

"This is no joke, Nick," Jericho said. "I want to meet Miss Barry at ten o'clock in the Palm Court. The only way to make sure of it is to tell you that if she isn't there—"

"Now wait a minute," Al said. "We can't—"

"Someone kidnaped Pat," Jericho said. "Some long-haired creeps—which suggests Ferrick. It occurred to me that Trans American Broadcasting and Helstrom Cosmetics might be able to persuade Don boy that it would be advisable to have Miss Barry at the Palm Court at ten o'clock. If she isn't there, then, alas, the Nolan paintings will not be available for the Zelda special tomorrow morning. Is that simple enough, or do you need it spelled out for you?"

"You can't do it," Glass said. "The paintings are all set up at the studio. They're an integral part of the background for the show. They're written into the script. You can't change your mind at this late date."

"Ten o'clock in the Palm Court," Jericho said. "You try to roll the cameras tomorrow morning without my permission and you'll find yourself slapped with an injunction that'll put you out of business for days."

"Can he do that?" Glass asked Al.

"He could," Al said.

"Then find Miss Barry and get her to the Palm Court at ten o'clock," Nick said. "So help me, if this turns out to be some sort of practical joke—"

"It's not a joke," Jericho said.

"Miss Barry can be found?" Glass asked Al.

"How the hell should I know, Nick?" Al said.

"I'm loaded with advice," Jericho said. "Let Al talk to Don Ferrick. Let Al tell him exactly what will happen to him if he doesn't deliver Miss Barry at ten o'clock."

"What will happen to him?" Glass asked.

"That's for you, Nick, representing a giant of communications, and somebody from Helstrom's, representing a giant of industry, to figure out. Maybe you can just buy him; maybe you can just twist his arm. But remember one thing. I need to be satisfied with the condition of the merchandise when it's delivered to me."

"You better move, Al," Glass said. "It's going on eight o'clock. You know where to find Ferrick?"

"Everybody knows where to find him at this time of day," Al said bitterly. . . .

I had that nice comfortable feeling that this particular piece of Jericho madness was over. I had faith in communications and cosmetics. I had been in on other climaxes with him in which I had come unpleasantly close to being a target. It was all over now, I told myself. No bones broken. No serious injuries. At ten o'clock Pat Barry

187

would come smiling across the Palm Court to where we were waiting for her. We'd go to my place and have a drink, even if it was only ten o'clock in the morning. Time had gotten a little turned around for all of us.

I was glad it had all come out so well because I was actually responsible for getting Jericho into the act to start with.

I was, it turned out, Johnny-Head-in-Air about to step into an open manhole.

Jericho and I walked across town to the Plaza. We weren't in a hurry. Jericho announced he was starving, and we went into the main dining room and were assigned to a table overlooking Central Park, gleaming in the early-morning sunlight. I had tomato juice, two boiled eggs, and a slice of dry toast. I'm always on a semi-diet. Jericho had a two-pound hunk of broiled sirloin, garnished with home-fried potatoes, grilled tomatoes, and fried onion rings.

When he had eaten a little of the steak, he relaxed. "I'm about to make you a promise, Hally," he said. "No more cops and robbers. So help me. I'm getting too old for it. My point of view is all wrong. I still believe in the Knights of the Round Table, Robin Hood, and the Scarlet Pimpernel. It's out of date. I am a painter. I will paint what I see. But I swear I will never again involve myself in the troubles of complete strangers."

"Good," I said. "Of course, there are still some loose ends to tie up here. Tommy Nolan was murdered. Was Perry really the intended victim? Who did it? Who tipped

188

off the police you were about to have your skull smashed in on a deserted subway platform? You owe that someone a polite thank you."

"I will leave it to you to express my gratitude. I couldn't care less who tried to kill Perry Lewis. Pascal will dig him out and polish him off. Starting from the moment she walks in here this morning, I am going to devote myself to giving Pat Barry the most marvelous time of her life. There's a little village in Spain I want her to see. There's a chalet high up in the Swiss Alps. There's a beach on a tiny island in the British West Indies. There's the little town in New England where I went to school, and a mountain camp high up in Colorado."

"The gal seems to have got her hooks into you," I said. Of course, he hadn't told me Pat's secret at that point.

"She has," he said crisply. "I'm going to show her that there's nothing like living life at a fast gallop. Advice to unhappily married couples!" He snorted.

At about a quarter past nine we paid our check and went out into the deserted Palm Court. This is a great tea-time gathering place for society ladies. It's a far more elegant version of the meeting place of my young years, under the clock at the Biltmore. Jericho made the reasonable comment that Pat might not be delivered at precisely ten. She could appear in advance of the deadline. Jericho sat for about eighty seconds, and then he began to pace restlessly up and down the corridor just off the court, chewing on the stem of his unlighted pipe.

Glass and Company were cutting it a little fine, I

thought, when my watch showed me it was six minutes to ten. Someone earlier in this charade had mentioned "the creeping hours of time." I was reminded of another quote from *As You Like It:*

> And so from hour to hour we ripe and ripe,
> And then from hour to hour we rot and rot;
> And thereby hangs a tale.

Jericho had rejoined me from his patrol of the corridor. His face was dark now, and I could see the muscles ripple along the line of his jaw under the red beard. It began to look as though it wasn't going to happen.

At two minutes to ten Maury Zimmerman, TAB's top salesman, appeared across the Palm Court, spotted us, and came on the run, like a Beagle hot on the trail.

"Let's sit down and talk things over," Maury said. He was on the breathless side.

Jericho just looked at his watch and kept looking.

"Even you two guys have to deal with reason now and then," Maury said, grinning at us. I don't think Maury believed there was any situation he couldn't talk his way out of or into as he pleased.

"You haven't got her," Jericho said grimly.

Maury pointed at me. "Tell him why," he said.

I just looked at him blankly.

"You did a profile on Zelda, didn't you, pal? You wrote all about what happens to her the day before a special performance or opening. You wrote about the special gimmick she has in her contract."

190

"A day in seclusion?" I remembered it.

"Right," Maury said. "In black and white. The day be-fore a big special, or an opening, she has the right to be unavailable. The director can't see her; the costume de-signer can't see her; no one connected with the show can bother her. Her privilege—in black and white. It is the time when she, shall we say, refreshes herself."

"So?" Jericho said.

"The party broke up at the Hell Hole about four this morning," Maury said. "Shortly thereafter Zelda, Perry, and Ferrick were whisked away by the chauffeur to a place of seclusion."

"Where?" Jericho asked.

"My dear old boy, I haven't the foggiest notion, and neither has anyone else connected with TAB or Helstrom Cosmetics. Nor does any reasonably close friend we've been able to contact. I am here to tell you that we have done everything humanly possible to comply with your demands. We haven't come even close by the deadline." He glanced up at a gold-framed clock in the lobby. It was one minute past ten. "All we can do is promise to keep try-ing. Someone must know various places where they've gone in the past. If I told you we had fifty people looking for them, would you be satisfied?"

"No," Jericho said.

"If I told you that once we do find Ferrick we've de-vised a way to make things intolerable for him unless he does what we ask—would that satisfy you?"

"What have you devised?"

Maury grinned. "Trade secret," he said. "Let me simply assure you that if Ferrick has it in his power to deliver Miss Barry, he will deliver."

"And if you don't find them?"

"They will appear tomorrow morning at the Brooklyn studios of TAB. That, too, is in black and white."

"Ferrick will appear?"

"He always has," Maury said.

"You realize that means Pat stays in the hands of a bunch of sadistic cannibals for another twenty-four hours?"

"There are girls who would cry for the chance," Maury said, grinning.

Jericho seemed to just touch Maury's chest with the tips of his fingers. Maury sat down very hard on the floor. His cheerful little face turned the color of ashes.

"God, I hate muscle men," he said quietly.

Jericho reached down and pulled him up to his feet. "I'm sorry," he said. "I've been pushed around so much myself in the last few hours it's gotten to be a habit."

Maury brushed at his suit. His cheerfulness was gone. "We're not giving up," he said. "We'll keep looking, and if we find him, we'll apply the treatment at once. All we ask is that you know that we're doing what we can, so don't throw injunctions at us till we've had a chance."

"Again, I'm sorry I pushed you," Jericho said.

"Let me know where you can be reached," Maury said, ignoring the apology.

I gave him my number. "We'll go there now," I said.

"See you around, God forbid!" Maury said, and walked quickly toward the Fifth Avenue doors of the hotel.

Jericho was muttering under his breath as we followed Maury out onto the street.

"I didn't mean to push him so hard!" he said. "He made a cheap crack about Pat. It was instinctive."

"He'll get over it," I said. "He'll realize how much heat there's been on all of us."

Jericho signaled a taxi. There was nothing to do but go to my place and wait. We had no trail to follow. Maybe Glass and Company would eventually locate Zelda. Our chances were zero.

My apartment is in an old brownstone down off Irving Place. I have the basement and the first floor, with a private entrance from the street. Before my time it had been a setup for a doctor. I opened the street door behind it. Jericho was paying off the taxi. I pushed the door open and stopped.

Someone was sitting on the floor inside the door, arms locked around pulled-up knees, head forward. Asleep!

It was Zelda. . . .

"I didn't know where else to wait," she said.

I must have pushed the door further in when I reacted to seeing her. It jammed against her foot and woke her. Jericho bent down, picked her up as if she were an infant, and put her on her feet.

"A small army of people are looking for you," he said.

"And I've been looking for you," she said. "Finally I decided just to wait here till somebody came. Boy, am I stiff!"

I got the inside door unlocked, and we all went into my living room.

"I'm glad you're here, Zelda," Jericho said, not waiting for any polite ceremonies. "I'm sorry for all your troubles, but I've got mine too. I'm interested in just one thing. Where's your friend Ferrick?"

The wide eyes with their false eyelashes looked up at him. She had changed out of her evening things into slacks and a pale-green angora sweater. Except for her eyes she seemed to have on no make-up. It accentuated the little-girl quality.

"I don't know where Don is," she said.

"I was given to understand that you and Don and Perry were driven off somewhere by Eddie shortly after four this morning?"

She nodded. "That's true enough."

"Then you know where he is!"

"I don't. I really don't," she said. "Could I sit down while I explain to you? I—I feel just a little woozy."

"There isn't time for explanations," he said, his voice rising. "I just want to know where—"

"For God's sake, Johnny, let her tell it her way," I said.

"All right!" he said. "All right! Only quick, baby."

She sank down into a corner of my couch. Her eyelids fluttered with fatigue. "We left our house because it was the only way to break up the party," she said. "I had to get some quiet. I have to get ready for tomorrow. We al-

194

ways do that the night before the day I take off. It's the only way we can get rid of people. Most always we come back in a while and just settle quietly into our own place again. We couldn't do that tonight. We knew there'd probably be the police and you, Jericho, and God knows who else demanding to see us. We thought we'd take a suite of rooms at a hotel, but I was certain the news would leak and there'd be people with questions and more questions. We were arguing in the car. Perry was screaming like a lunatic that no place was safe for him—accusing me, accusing Don of trying to kill him. He was wild. I had to have quiet! I had to get pulled together! So I told Eddie to stop the car and I got out and I told them they could go where they pleased. I *had* to be alone. They drove off."

"And left you standing on the street corner?"

She nodded. "It wasn't anything very new. It had happened before. We argue and fight and then I get out of whatever we're in—the car or a taxi—and that's that. Mostly I go back to the house and they go off and burn up the town somewhere."

"Where?"

"There are all kinds of bottle clubs and other dives that go full blast all day Sunday if you know where to find them," she said. "I couldn't tell you where because I don't know. I never go with them on those outings."

"Did you go back to your house?"

"No." She smiled, a puzzled little smile. "There's a funny thing about me. I can't not answer the phone. If it rings, I have to answer it. Even in the middle of—well, in the middle of anything, no matter how important, if the phone rings, I have to answer it. I knew if I went home the phone would be ringing and I wouldn't have any quiet."

That, I knew, was the truth. When I'd been interviewing her for the profile, the phone was a disaster. I'd finally persuaded her to come to my place where we could talk, uninterrupted. That's how she knew where I lived.

"So you came here to be quiet?" Jericho said, his anger rising again.

"Not exactly," she said.

He turned away from her impatiently. "Pascal must know about these bottle clubs and Sunday dives," he said. He strode off to the phone in my study.

"It doesn't sound reasonable, does it?" she said to me in a very small voice. "Talking about needing quiet and a chance to get pulled together before tomorrow, and then coming here where all the trouble is."

"There's Patricia Barry," I said. "We've got to find her." I told her about TAB and Helstrom both on Ferrick's trail. "There isn't going to be any show, Zelda, unless she turns up safe and sound."

She leaned her head back against the couch, and the long lashes closed over her eyes. "I ought not to care," she said.

"Whether there is a show or not?"

"Whether Patricia Barry turns up safe and sound," she said, without opening her eyes. When I didn't speak they popped open. "I'm sorry, Hally," she said. "I got so used to talking to you when you were doing the profile that things just come out—like you were my best friend. You see, if it wasn't for Patricia Barry, Tommy Nolan would be alive today."

I heard a sharp intake of breath behind me and knew that Jericho had come back into the room, but I didn't turn.

"I don't follow you," I said to Zelda.

"I have to hate her for that," Zelda said.

"Are you trying to say Pat tried to kill Perry and Nolan drank the poison instead?" Jericho asked from behind me. "Pat wasn't at your place that night. She told me."

"Oh, it wasn't anything as direct as that," Zelda said. "You see, if it hadn't been for Patricia Barry, Tommy and I would have gone off somewhere together, and so he wouldn't have been around to get the poison by mistake."

"You and Nolan?"

"You'd probably laugh, Jericho. You heard me sing. It's probably nothing to you."

"I told you it was wonderfully good," he said.

"You were probably just being a nice guy," she said. "But to me, when I'm singing is the only time I'm the real me. The rest is all something I wish I wasn't. When I sing, I am talking to people, only nobody answers back. If you see what I mean. It's a one-way conversation with appreciation from the listener but no talking back. But Tommy Nolan could talk back—with his pictures. We were a natural, Tommy and me. But I was tied up to Perry and to

197

Don, and I was a rotten kind of a person, and Tommy was tied up to Patricia Barry. She doesn't know it, but she's going to die pretty soon. Some kind of blood cancer. And Tommy wouldn't leave her."

"She knows it," Jericho said. "He didn't know it."

"Her doctor told him," Zelda said. "She talks in her sleep. Kind of scary to think of, isn't it, considering who you might be sleeping with? So, anyway, he wouldn't leave her. When she was gone, then we were planning to go somewhere and talk to each other forever. Only he drank what was meant for Perry. So you see, if it hadn't been for her, we'd have been long gone and he wouldn't be dead."

Her eyes closed and a little shudder ran over her body.

"She doesn't deserve what may be happening to her," Jericho said. "That's why I've got to get her back, Zelda, and quick. I promised her the time she had left would be a good time, and then I let this happen to her."

Zelda's eyes opened. "Is she why you said no to me?"

"No. Did you know that your dressing room at the Barber Pole Club was bugged? Perry played back our conversation to me on a tape recorder."

She shrugged. "I'm used to that," she said. "So I just say what I think and to hell with him. He's a nut for gadgets. He should have been a character in a James Bond story. The car has all sorts of crazy stuff in it. He's got a workshop in the basement where he invents things—like stink bombs he dropped in the Metropolitan Opera one night, noisemakers, and God knows what. He's like that nutty

198

character in *You Can't Take It with You*, only mean."

I glanced at Jericho. His face was hard. I knew we were both wondering the same thing. There had been a home-made bomb and some kind of explosive gadget for blowing the lock off Pascal's door. Was Zelda using this rambling technique to tell us something?

"Why did you come here, Zelda?" I asked. "You didn't really come here to look for quiet."

"I came to beg you for a favor," she said.

"Try us," I said.

"There's a new song I'm doing in the special," she said. "Tommy Nolan wrote the words. It's called "Reaching For I Don't Know What." There's a painting of his—"

"I know it," Jericho said.

"The song says everything to the goofy people in the world, like me, and the lost screwpots like Don Ferrick and all his friends, and the hollow-eyed kids on the street. It tells them no matter who laughs at you, or clubs you, or jerks you off your spot and puts a gun in your hand to kill a neighbor—a black neighbor, or a yellow neighbor, or even a white neighbor—you've got to remember to keep reaching, even if you don't know exactly what you're reaching for. You've got to keep reaching for some kind of something that means Truth to you." She drew a deep breath. "It opens the show. I want to sing it. I want it down on film, with Tommy's painting there beside me, so that all the thousands and thousands of people it was meant for will get to hear it—no matter what happens."

"What do you mean—no matter what happens?"

She looked steadily at Jericho. "This special is never going to be finished. I feel it in my bones. You won't let it, Jericho; the police won't let it, and in the end the network and the client won't let it. But I want that one song done—the first in the show. And I want to see to it that somehow it gets to the people it was meant for."

"Tell me how to get Pat Barry away from Ferrick."

"I can't," Zelda said, turning her head from side to side. "I don't know how. I don't know where Don is." She leaned forward. "Let me stay here. You can use me as a hostage against her. You want her safe because you like her. They all want me safe because I'm their meal ticket. Use me against them any way you want, but let me get that first number sung before you throw the switch on me."

"If you're trying to protect Ferrick, if you're giving him time to get away," Jericho said, "if you're a partner in what happens to Pat, so help me, Zelda, I'll run you through a very fine meat grinder."

"I'm here—unless you drive me away," she said. She looked at me. "Is there a place I could get some sleep, Hally? I'm dead on my feet."

# Five

A day and a night can pass like lightning when you're in love, or perhaps in the death house.

It was just a little before noon when I showed Zelda to the guest room on the second floor of my apartment. The windows opened out onto a city garden, brave and dirty. Jericho and I settled down to wait and think, because that was all there was to do. We drank a little and ate a little when we felt like it.

And Zelda slept through the day and into the night.

There were periodic phone calls. One from Pascal told us that there were dozens of these so-called Sunday joints. The whole damned city seemed to be bent on Sunday carousing. No trace of Ferrick. No word of Perry Lewis. Maury Zimmerman called once, and later Al Stover. They were doing their best, but the results were negative.

About six o'clock Nick Glass called. He had to know

what Jericho was going to do. Zelda was due at the studio at eight-thirty in the morning for make-up and costume. The cameras were scheduled to roll at ten. The least Jericho could do would be to tell them if he was going to produce a court order.

"It all depends," Jericho said. "If Ferrick is there, and he can produce Miss Barry—"

"Oh God!" Glass said.

Partly answered questions went round and round in my head. There were so many people who hated Perry who could have poisoned his jug. The attitude of Ferrick and his friends had been made fairly clear by Herman Melville and Charles Dickens. Now we could guess where they'd come by a bomb and special explosives on the spur of the moment. Perry's passion for gadgets and his workshop, easily available to Ferrick, explained that. But who had tipped off the police and spoiled Ferrick's total revenge on the subway platform?

Jericho had told me briefly the story of Pat Barry's illness, which had come again from Zelda, with the peculiar twist that Tommy Nolan had known—and that Tommy Nolan and Zelda had themselves been a "thing," but a kind of a thing totally unlike anything else in Zelda's twisted life.

I know the thing Jericho couldn't get out of his mind was the almost intolerable imagining of what might be happening to Pat. There was no way to guess at a pattern of behavior for Ferrick and his Regency boys. They might be treating Pat with elaborate courtesy; they might be subjecting her to God knows what kind of deviated mental and physical agony.

And there was literally nothing we could do but sit and wait while the hours crept by.

And then from hour to hour we rot and rot . . .

Zelda had slept around the clock before I heard her stirring. She came out into the living room, which was thick with the acrid blue smoke from Jericho's endless pipe smoking. Her eyes were puffed, like a child's, with sleep. We told her there was no news.

She was hungry, and while I made her a sandwich and poured her a glass of cold milk, she talked about the coming day's work, as though there was nothing else. She talked about Jimmy Cooper, the pianist who made all her arrangements, and what a doll he was; she talked with genuine respect about Rich Ragsdale, who, despite his sardonic attitudes, was really a very great pro; she talked about Perry.

"He is really a very great bastard," she said casually, "but there are good things to say for him. His methods drive people like Al Stover crazy, but he's really handled my career without a mistake. There are only a couple of people in the business who can command more money than I can—Bob Hope and maybe Barbra Streisand. You have to hand that to Perry."

"You hand it to him," Jericho growled from the armchair where he sat, beard sunk forward on his chest.

She would have to leave for the Brooklyn studios not

later than seven-thirty in the morning, she told us. The commuter traffic would be heavy. She had to be in the hands of the make-up man by eight-thirty. And then she went to bed, as though the world was rotating on a perfectly normal course.

I doubt if Jericho slept at all. I slept very little.

And there was no easing word from anyone as to the whereabouts of Don Ferrick. . . .

We arrived at the Trans American studios the next morning at a quarter past eight. We were confronted by a strange combination of total efficiency and madhouse.

One whole floor of the studio was to be used for the special. It was already in command of Rich Ragsdale and his camera, stage, and lighting crews. Set pieces were carefully placed. A couple of dozen of Tommy Nolan's paintings, carefully covered, were ready for use. A girl, vaguely like Zelda in size and appearance, was standing under the lights, moving from place to place, while Ragsdale, behind the glass front of the control booth, talked with his floor manager and the other technicians on the intercom system, checking and rechecking. The four cameras and their crews moved in and out of position, in a sort of dry run. Voices were calm. These were men who knew their jobs.

Zelda had gone straight to the star's dressing room where the make-up man and her dresser waited for her. Nobody asked questions. All these people seemed to know exactly what the next move was.

We were ushered into a sort of reception room behind the control booth, and there the atmosphere was something else again. Jericho had hardly stepped through the door when he was surrounded by Nick Glass, Al Stover, Farmer and Crowley, the P.R. men, and the stone-faced Max Morrison, Helstrom's legal beagle. What was Jericho going to do? Were they to be allowed to proceed? The simple truth was they hadn't been able to find Don Ferrick. So far he hadn't come to the studio.

Jericho brushed them aside. His attention was focused on Perry Lewis, who was perched on a window seat across the room, a drink of some kind in one hand, and that machine pistol with its ugly-looking silencer across his knees. He was grinning like some kind of evil gnome. Jericho went straight over to him.

"I see you finally did take Zelda up on her offer," Perry said. "Worth it?"

Jericho ignored the comment and the question. "Where's Ferrick?" he asked.

"How the hell should I know?" Perry said.

"He's your bodyguard."

"A man would be a fool to continue being guarded by someone who wants him dead," Perry said. "We parted company—I may say forever—early yesterday morning. Zelda may not like it, but that's the way it is."

"Unless we find him and he delivers Pat Barry to me, there isn't going to be any show," Jericho said.

Perry's grin was maddening. "My, my," he said. "Of course I couldn't care less. Zelda and I are ready. If someone else stops the show, we've fulfilled our part of the deal."

"What can you gain by stopping us, Jericho?" Glass asked. "It won't find you Ferrick. We've done and will continue to do everything we can."

"Your quarrel with this man Ferrick has nothing whatever to do with this filming," the lawyer with the stone face said. "I doubt very much you can make any legal action stick, my friend."

I knew Jericho had taken no action. If they wanted to go, they could go, at least for the moment.

Jericho turned to Glass. "You make the decision," he said. "I promise you this. I can smear this whole operation from one end to the other so that you can never show the film you make, and I will if Miss Barry isn't very quickly delivered. Run the risk if you like."

You could almost see the dollar signs dancing in front of Nick Glass's eyes. He was sweating, in spite of the air conditioning. Finally he turned to Al Stover. "Tell Ragsdale it's his baby. He can roll."

"I must wish my beloved wife well," Perry said, as Al Stover headed for the control booth. "I must also provide her with her good-luck charm." He limped away, carrying his drink—and his gun.

Jericho looked at me. "What else?" he said. "At least this way we know where everyone is."

Marty Farmer, the P.R. man for TAB, gave us a kind of frozen smile. "You might as well watch from the control booth," he said.

He opened the door and we went in. Ragsdale turned impatiently. "Oh, it's you," he said to Jericho. "Sit down over there and keep quiet."

There were Ragsdale and his assistant director and four men sitting in front of the four monitors, each of which would show on its screens the actions of each of the four cameras.

Ragsdale adjusted his headphones. Out on the floor Zelda's stand-in was sitting in a small straight-backed chair under the lights. One of the monitors showed her clearly. The second monitor showed Tommy Nolan's painting of the reaching girl. It stood on an easel four or five feet away from the stand-in.

Ragsdale clicked the intercom button and spoke to the people out on the floor.

"Ask Miss Rankin to come out for a minute," he said. Then: "We'll begin at the top of the show, fellows," he said. "Zelda will do her reaching number and then we'll segue into the second song. I want to try the silhouette business. You ready, Perry?"

Perry's voice came from some hidden place. "Ready, sire."

"We'll just try the mechanics once," Ragsdale said. "Miss Johnson, you're in the position where Zelda finishes her number. As the last note ends, you back slowly to the chair and sit down. The screen comes down and you go off, unseen. Then we see the silhouette of Perry's figure come on behind the screen and take away the chair. You there, Zelda?"

"Here," Zelda's voice answered from a place I couldn't see.

"Let's just walk through it," Ragsdale said. "Lights?"

"Ready, Rich."

"Music take the last eight bars," Ragsdale said. "In place, Miss Johnson."

What I saw and heard went something like this. The music began and Miss Johnson stood silent, her head raised. I glanced at the monitors. One camera was on Miss Johnson. Another was on Nolan's painting. The music came to an end. Miss Johnson took two steps back and eased gently down into the chair.

"Screen!" Ragsdale said. "Cameras three and four!"

A white, silky-looking curtain came down in front of Miss Johnson and the paintings. The lights changed in some subtle fashion. Then a silhouetted figure appeared behind the silk screen. We could see the chair. The figure limped over to the chair, picked it up, and walked off with it.

"Lights!" Ragsdale said.

Again the lights changed. The silk screen evaporated, and there was Miss Johnson on another side of the stage walking slowly in front of a simulated exhibition of Nolan's paintings.

"Cut," Ragsdale said. "Perfect, boys. Any questions, Zelda?"

"None."

"When you're ready then, sweetheart. Any problems, Perry?"

208

"My drink is empty," Perry said.

The intercom clicked. "Sonofabitch," Ragsdale said cheerfully. Nobody outside the booth could hear him. "We do this early so he will be sober," he added, looking at us.

"I don't get it," I said.

"A superstition borrowed from Hitchcock," Ragsdale said. "Perry must appear somewhere in each show of Zelda's. That's his appearance, unsung and unannounced, removing that chair. After we shoot it he can go home—I hope."

A few moments later the floor manager's voice came over the intercom. "Zelda's ready, Rich."

"I'm ready when you are," Ragsdale said. "Have fun."

"Quiet in the booth, please," someone said.

"Lights, cameras, and music ready, Rich," the floor manager said.

"Roll," Rich said. "Music—"

A cone of light suddenly came from straight overhead, illuminating the chair, with Zelda sitting on it in her simple white dress. The music was eerie. I thought there was a concertina, a flute, a plucked bass-rhythmic. Zelda turned her head and looked at the picture of the reaching girl on the easel. I couldn't watch the monitors to see how it would eventually look at home. I couldn't listen to Ragsdale's orders: "Take One . . . Take Three . . ." Slowly Zelda rose and walked over to the painting. And then she began to sing. It was the song she'd described to us. "*No matter who laughs at you, no matter who clubs*

*you . . . keep reaching . . . for that something . . .
that means Truth to you . . ."*

I felt a little cold finger run along my spine. Jericho was
right. This girl could make magic. I heard Ragsdale mut-
ter under his breath, "Jesus, she's good!"

The song ended on a high, clear note. The music
faded except for the flute, fading into the distance. Zelda
stepped back and sat slowly in the chair, the bright cone
of light beating down on her. The silvery-white curtain
came slowly down. The lights changed so that all we saw
was the silhouetted figure crossing behind the curtain,
picking up the chair, and going off. The music came back
in a new melody. The silvery curtain rose. The lights were
suddenly bright on the simulated art gallery showing
Nolan's paintings. But Zelda wasn't there.

"What the hell . . . !" Ragsdale said.

Then the floor manager's voice came over the intercom,
high and a little shaken. "I'm afraid we can't go on, Rich,"
he said. "I think Perry has shot himself." . . .

Perry Lewis was very dead. He had taken the full blast
of the machine pistol from very close up. He was
sprawled on the floor beside a chair, his right hand still on
the gun. I suppose someone had sent for the police, but
for the moment Jericho seemed automatically to be in
charge—he had assumed it. He and I and Ragsdale and
the floor manager, a fellow named Shanley, stood around
the body. Zelda had been taken to her dressing room, and
Shanley had his floor crew keeping everyone else away,

including a clamoring Nick Glass.

The floor of the studio created a very different picture from what we had seen from the booth. The place where Perry lay was a narrow little corner made by flats and draperies.

"We couldn't see him," Shanley kept saying. "Ordinarily I would have given him the cue to go on behind the silver cloth when his time came. It couldn't be done, so we figured a way to time it perfectly. Zelda had to come off, and so she just touched him on the shoulder when she was clear of the camera, and he came on."

"Where did she go after she gave him his cue?" Jericho asked.

"Back of those flats and across stage to the library set."

"You didn't hear a shot?"

"Silencer," the floor manager said.

"This is being filmed," Jericho said. "Why didn't you simply break and pick up again?"

"I wanted this particular segue to be all part of one piece of action," Ragsdale said. "Once we picked Zelda up walking through the gallery set, we'd cut and get ready for the next musical number."

Somebody had covered Perry's mangled face with a sheet.

"Is it possible to get an instant playback of what you just finished shooting?" Jericho said.

"Sure," Ragsdale said.

"Let's go look," Jericho said.

I couldn't guess what he was driving at, but his tired

eyes were suddenly very bright. We all went back to the control booth and Ragsdale spoke to someone on the phone.

"You can start just before the end of the song," Jericho said.

We waited in silence. Then Ragsdale indicated the center monitor. The screen sputtered and popped for a minute and suddenly Zelda was singing to us—the last few bars of the reaching song. It ended, and she backed up and sat down in the chair. The lights changed. The silver drape came down. And then the silhouetted figure moved across behind it and took away the chair.

"That's it," Jericho said.

Ragsdale switched off the monitor, and he and I sat looking at Jericho. Slowly Jericho turned to us.

"You didn't see it?" he asked.

"See what?" Ragsdale asked.

"A whole man can imitate a lame man without any trouble," Jericho said. "But a lame man can't imitate a whole man."

We just looked at him, still not getting it.

"The silhouetted figure on your film, Ragsdale, didn't limp. It couldn't have been Perry. He couldn't walk without a limp."

"But—"

"If Perry was shot after he made his cross to take away the chair, it couldn't have been Zelda," Jericho said. "She'd have been in the library set by then. But if he was shot *before* his time for crossing came, then Zelda must have known it when she touched him to give him his cue. Then who crossed for Perry? Zelda would know that too. She hasn't come forward with information." Jericho shrugged. "I'm sorry. Everybody has a breaking point."

Zelda sat in front of the mirror in her dressing room. She didn't turn as we came in. She saw Jericho in the mirror and she very slowly put down the tissue with which she'd been wiping some make-up lines from her forehead.

"You figured it," she said without emotion.

Jericho nodded without speaking. I closed the dressing-room door on the curious crew that were milling about in the corridor.

"I thought I'd fixed myself a perfect alibi," she said.

"You forgot to limp," Jericho said.

Her eyes widened. "You wouldn't think I could forget that limp, would you? It had to be done so fast—"

"I'm sorry."

She laughed, an edgy laugh. "Go home, Johnny boy," she said. "Your girl friend should be there waiting for you by now." She turned slowly to face us. "I wish, just once in my life, someone had given me the kind of kid-glove treatment she's had the last hours."

"Where is she?" Jericho asked, his voice harsh.

"I tell you, on her way to Hally's place. She'll be waiting for you when you get there. It's a laugh, isn't it? She made trouble for me with Tommy and trouble for me in this last little horseplay, and she comes out of it without a scar. Me—well, nothing ever really worked for me."

She turned away to stare at herself in the mirror. She could have been looking at a stranger. Instinctively we knew she'd have to tell it her own way, and finally she began to talk—sounding as though she couldn't quite believe it herself.

"Tommy Nolan was where it all began," she said. Her lips quivered slightly. "I would have done anything for him, gone anywhere he asked, given up anything he wanted me to give up. And do you know, he never even touched me, never even kissed me just for the hell of it. When I was with him, I was like what I'd always wanted to be and never could. Perry saw how it was, that I was ready to run out on him. He couldn't afford to lose me. He couldn't afford to lose the power my position in show business gave him—and my money gave him. Power was everything to him."

"Wasn't he afraid you'd run away with Don Ferrick some day?" Jericho asked. "You told me the kind of physical hold Ferrick has on you."

She shuddered. "That was different. Don couldn't help me with my career. He isn't clever enough. He's all animal behind a phony front. Don couldn't do anything for me except satisfy a craving I had for what he can give. I'd never have walked out on my career for Don. But Tommy Nolan? I would. I swear I would have. And so—Perry killed him."

Her mouth twitched. "It took me a day or three to realize it. Like you, I thought that poisoned jug had been meant for Perry. And then it came clear to me. It wasn't

214

an accident. Perry meant all along for Tommy to drink what was in that jug. All along it was murder, planned by Perry, worked by Perry. If the suicide theory didn't stick, well, then he'd make it apparent that the attack had been meant for him. When you came into the picture, Jericho, he decided you were dangerous, might guess the truth. He had to get rid of you or persuade you the poison had been meant for him."

"And I played right into his hands—with Ferrick," Jericho said.

She nodded. "He was delighted by your quarrel with Don. He kept stoking the fires of Don's rage at you for making him look foolish. He specialized in gadgets in his workshop and he had that homemade bomb there. He goaded Don into using it. Don is the kind of a madman who would buy an idea like that. When that didn't work and you weren't scared off, it was Perry who suggested snatching the girl. The idea amused Perry. 'Turn her loose in a pack of sex-crazy longhairs,' he suggested to Don. So Don and his friends snatched her.

"It was just about then I realized what was going on and why. I managed to show Don what would happen to him if the girl was harmed. Perry would turn on him, show the cops that Don was responsible for the bombing, the kidnaping, and also of an attempt to murder him— Perry—using me as the reason. Don could be in a very bad corner. Don listened, but he couldn't forget about you, Jericho. He had to get even with you, no matter how I pleaded with him and told him how dangerous it would be. So he arranged the thing on the subway platform and —and I tipped the cops."

"It was a man who called the police!" Jericho said.

She laughed. "Didn't you ever hear my imitations?" she said in a suddenly deep, clearly male voice.

Jericho didn't move a muscle.

"Last night I thought a lot about it," she said. She looked the puzzled little girl for a moment. "Perry had to be punished. I could go to the police, but Perry would then turn the whole thing against Don, and I didn't think I could prove he was lying. I wanted Perry to pay, and I wanted him to know I was making him pay. I wanted Don safe. He was all I had left in this cockeyed world.

"So I told Don what I was going to do, and I made him promise to turn your Miss Barry loose at eleven o'clock this morning. I knew I would kill Perry in that first scene in the special—where I could alibi myself. Perry had acted out his pretended fear that someone was trying to get him. I thought I could act out my shock at his suicide —because I thought you'd all buy it as suicide." She laughed. "A lame brain, Perry used to call me. A lame brain who forgot to limp!" She rocked gently back and forth. Then she looked up, and I thought her eyes didn't quite focus. "How did you like the song?" she asked.

"It was great," Jericho said.

"If Tommy had written the words long ago, I—I might have started reaching soon enough to miss all this. If it could only be heard, Johnny. If all the crazy, lost, mixed-up kids like me could hear it—"

"I'll do my best," Jericho said.

"I'll bet you will," she said. "You're like Tommy was, you know? You believe in crazy kinds of things." She turned away, not looking at us. "Go find your girl, Johnny. And give her a good time—in the time she has. She's lucky. It would be fun to have fun for just a few months. Then I wouldn't care what they do to me. How bad will it be, Johnny?"

"Bad," he said quietly.

"You would tell the truth," she said. "Tommy was that way too. It was kind of a new experience for me—and look where it's got me!"